Strangers in Stickleback Hollow

The Mysteries of Stickleback Hollow®

Book 23

By C.S. Woolley

A Mightier Than the Sword UK Publication

©2025

Strangers in Stickleback Hollow
The Mysteries of Stickleback Hollow®

By C. S. Woolley

A Mightier Than the Sword UK Publication

Paperback Edition

ISBN Kindle 978-1-991125-47-7
ISBN Paperback 978-1-991125-46-0

For

Karl

The Mysteries of Stickleback Hollow® - Strangers in Stickleback Hollow

Author's Note

Thanks for taking the time to read Strangers in Stickleback Hollow, this book was something of a surprise when the idea for it came to me and actually opened the floodgates for a whole host of other stories that fall outside the original narrative.

As this book was a surprise, I wanted to dedicate it to another great surprise in my life - a friend who came into my life most unexpectedly and turned everything on its head in the best possible way. You have been an unexpected source of support and help that I could not do without.

The last year of my life, and yours, have not been the easiest or best, but somehow you manage to be supportive, kind, and stern when called for. Your support truly is invaluable, and I couldn't do all of this without you having my back.

Thank you for your support, your belief, and just for being

you! You are more appreciated than I can ever express!

Kia Kaha.

The Characters

Lady Sarah Montgomery Baird Watson-Wentworth
The heroine
Mr Alexander Hunter Webb-Kneelingroach
A huntsman and heir to Grangeback Estate
Constable Arwyn Evans
Policeman in Stickleback Hollow
Sylvia Lennox
Lady Sarah's Companion and Lady's Maid.
Pattinson
An Akita, Alexander's hunting dog
Stanley & Lee Baker
Sons of Miss Baker, wards and apprentices to Lady Sarah
Brigadier George Webb-Kneelingroach
Lord of Grangeback, Father of Alexander, & Lady Sarah's Guardian
Constable Thompson Buckley
Policeman in Stickleback Hollow
Mr Oliver Henry Brown
An American Gentleman
Doctor Jack Hales
Doctor in Stickleback Hollow
Richard Hales
Trainee doctor and son of Jack Hales
Thomas Egerton
A gentleman of Cheshire, one of the Egerton's of Tatton Park
Edward Egerton
A gentleman of Cheshire, one of the Egerton's of Tatton Park
Charles & Charlotte Egerton
The Egerton twins, the youngest children of the Egerton family

Wilson
Owner and barkeep at Wilson's Inn
Emma
Owner and cook at Wilson's Inn
Muriel
Cook at Duffleton Hall
Mrs Hubbard
Housekeeper at Duffleton Hall
Fortesque
Butler at Duffleton Hall
The Honourable Mr Wilbraham Egerton
Owner of Tatton Park
Mrs Elizabeth Egerton née Sykes
Wife of Wilbraham
Mr William Egerton M.P.
Member of Parliament for Cheshire North, son of Wilbraham and Elizabeth
Lady Charlotte Elizabeth Egerton née Loftus
Wife of William
Mr Thomas Egerton
Son of Wilbraham & Elizabeth
Mrs Charlotte Egerton née Milner
Wife of Thomas
Mr Edward Christopher Egerton
Son of Wilbraham & Elizabeth
Miss Mary Pierrepont
Fiancée of Edward

August 1841

Chapter 1

Stickleback Hollow was not a place where people went for weeks without speaking to one another. In fact, if it was more than a few days since someone had been seen, a full scale alarm was raised.

The village would not rest until they knew where the individual was. It was one of the quirks of village life. Those that found it unnecessary and invasive did not stay in the village for long.

Some had managed to carve out something akin to privacy in the village, which meant that they could go five days to a week before people began to worry. Mostly these people were those who lived at Grangeback Manor and Duffleton Hall. The staff were often so busy that they were not seen until Sunday at church, or sometimes in Wilson's Inn for their night off.

So when Mr Oliver Henry Brown had not been seen for a week, people began to worry. None more so than Lady Sarah Montgomery Baird Watson Wentworth.

It had been a number of months since her engagement to Mr Alexander Hunter Webb-Kneelingroach had been announced, and she was concerned his absence was her fault.

Mr Hunter and Mr Brown have been in competition for the lady's heart for quite some time, and it had taken her many months to finally make a decision about whom she wished to marry. She had told Mr Brown of her decision to marry Mr Hunter before she accepted his proposal, out of respect for their friendship, and he had been gracious in her rejection.

Mr Brown had seemingly taken the engagement well. He had attended their engagement party, and even helped to solve a mystery of her ladyship's poisoning during the feast.

Since then, he had been rarely seen in the village, and his visits to Grangeback Manor had stopped altogether. He had retreated within the walls of Duffleton Hall, and not even been seen walking through the fields around his property.

To say that Lady Lady Sarah was concerned was an understatement.

After a week of him not being seen by anyone in the village, and his own staff reporting they had not seen him, she began to write letters to the American gentleman. Her messages were inquiring after his health, wondering if there was anything that they those at Grangeback Manor could do for him, etc.

When no response came, she sent yet more and more letters, each becoming more forceful in wanting to know what had happened to him, where he was, what he was doing, and why he was not answer.

Having sent multiple messages to Duffleton Hall, there was still no response over a period of yet another week, so Lady Sarah decided to call upon him unannounced.

Her companion, Sylvia, decided to accompany her there. Her fiancé felt she was being rather foolish in rushing to see if the man was all right.

"My darling, he was dealt a stinging blow when you accepted me over him. I suspect that though he has saved some amount of face by attending the party, and showing the world that he can carry on without you, he is feeling your loss most keenly. It would be best to let him be; to deal with his emotions in private," Mr Hunter had said very gently to his fiancée.

Lady Sarah disagreed.

"No. This feels different, it feels like there is something very wrong," she argued, and would not be swayed from journeying to Duffleton Hall.

Her companion, Sylvia, had only been too pleased to accompany her on a walk through the village to see whether anyone had seen him, before they called at the manor house.

It had been a while since they had walked out together on their own. Now that she was engaged, Mr Hunter had taken to accompanying Lady Sarah almost everywhere she went, as well as Sylvia, and though Sylvia did not mind the slight change in their routine, she did miss the times that they had spent together on their own.

They decided to walk down and begin where all people, at one point or another, in Stickleback Hollow would end up - Wilson's Inn. Wilson's Inn was a fine tavern to drink in. It had comfortable rooms for travelers who might pass through the village, and the most respectable place outside of the great houses within the vicinity of the village to eat.

It was run by Wilson and his wife, Emma Wilson.

What Wilson's first name was, only Emma seemed to know. But it did not matter to the people of Stickleback Hollow what his name was. Wilson was good enough for them at that was that.

Emma's cooking more than made-up for any mystery that might surround the older ageing man. Indeed, outside of Cooky at Grangeback Manor, Emma Wilson was considered to be the finest chef in the county.

That was a matter of debate with other people from other villages, but as far as the people of Stickleback Hollow were concerned. There was no one finer than Emma and Cooky when it came to food.

Wilson's Inn was rather quiet as they arrived that morning. The guests had all checked out, and Emma was busy creating the lunch dish that would be served to visitors in need of feeding at midday.

Wilson was cleaning the bar and ensuring that the rooms were neat and tidy for those guests that would be arriving later that day,

Stickleback Hollow was an out of the way sort of place. There were beautiful, walks through the forest, as well as other events that drew people to the village at all times of year, not just during that festival period. So many houses, being in such close proximity to the village meant that people came from far and wide to see the place.

The public were admitted to both houses to certain rooms at certain times of day, and Mrs Bosworth had always ensured anyone visiting Grangeback Manor were not seen by Lady Sarah, the brigadier, Sylvia, or Mr Hunter.

It was a little bit harder for her to keep. Guests at the hall, away from the general public. But Mrs Bosworth did her best in that regard.

"Good morning, Wilson," Lady Sarah greeted the barman, as she and Sylvia entered.

"Ah, your ladyship! What brings you down here on this fine day? I would not have expected to see you for a week at least," Wilson replied.

"We are going to call on Mr Brown, but we decided to find out if anyone in the village had seen him recently first," Lady Sarah smiled.

"I see. No surprise that you started here. No, not seen hide nor hair of him," he replied with a frown. "I had not thought about it before now, but it is rather odd I have not seen him walking about. He would normally just call in for a drink or two after he had been to Grangeback, but I suppose your engagement may have stopped him walking that way, changed his routine somewhat," Wilson said thoughtfully. "Can I offer you ladies a drink before you set off again on your task?"

"No, but we will call back before we return to the manor," Lady Sarah replied.

"Very good, ladies. I will ensure there is something suitable waiting for you," Wilson grinned.

It did not happen often, but Lady Sarah did enjoy gin and tonic. Growing up in India, and the fact that she had seen her parents drinking it, and all of their friends on a regular basis, gin and tonic had naturally been her first choice of alcoholic beverage. But for the most part, she drank tea.

There was the occasional snort of whiskey when it was offered at the manor. However, she found that alcohol clouded her mind too much, and since trouble seemed to find her wherever she went it was best to have a clear mind as often as possible.

After failing to find any news of Mr Brown at the inn, Lady Sarah and Sylvia made their way to Mr Pick, the green grocer, then on to the butcher, Miss Baker, the seamstress. After Miss Baker, they went to the baker himself. None had seen hide nor hair of Oliver.

In fact, everywhere Lady Sarah went, the answer was the same. Mr Brown had not been seen, and most had made the assumption that he was home, avoiding the village to try and save face in the wake of his failed attempts to secure her ladyship's hand in marriage.

The last place that the ladies went to before trying Duffleton Hall was the police house. Constable Arwyn Evans and Constable Thompson Buckley were the two local policemen.

Constable Buckley was new to the area, but he was settling in well, and proving, finally, to be the policeman that the village had needed after so many had proven to be less than suitable.

After all, those coming to the village to commit murder and kidnapping were probably not the best choice for police officers.

Constable Evans was surprised to see Lady Sarah at the police house, and immediately leapt to his feet, fearing the worst. As mostly, when she came calling, there was a mystery to be solved.

In fact, aside from the great events that took place annually around the village, there was little to share socially between her ladyship and the constable.   They were still good friends, despite this, but mostly they solved cases and mysteries together.

It was this that formed the majority of their friendship, so the sight of her often made Constable Evans believe that something terrible was happening.

"Your ladyship, this is a surprise," he said, leaping to his feet. "What? What's happened? What is it?"

"I do not know that anything has happened yet. No, indeed. But there is some concern. So there's that," Lady Sarah said, her thoughts slightly cluttered.

"What kind of concern?" Constable Buckley asked as he slowly lifted himself from his chair.

"Mr Brown. No one has seen him. It has been a few weeks now, but the last thing anyone saw of him was after the business at the engagement package," Lady Sarah replied.

'Her ladyship does not think, perhaps, he is just taking some time away from the village. Some time to lick his wounds before showing his face again?" Constable Buckley smiled. Lady Sarah sighed, and Sylvia smirked slightly.

"Surprisingly, as that has been everyone's suggestion since we first began doing this, including Mr Hunters. I have considered it," she said rather shortly.

The constable blushed slightly.

"Apologies, my lady. I forgot who I was talking to," Constable Buckley said and fell silent.

Sylvia tried not to laugh. She liked the constable but he had needed a slight rebuff for stating the obvious, even if Lady Sarah had been rather more harsh than Thompson Buckley deserved.

"You sent letters, but have you been to call on him yet?" Constable Evans asked, trying to divert attention away from Constable Buckley's embarrassment.

"No we are going there now. I am concerned," Lady Sarah said. "I can understand him not wishing to speak to me, but to disappear from the region entirely, that seems to be extraordinarily odd to me," Lady Sarah shrugged.

"Indeed, I would agree," Arwyn said pointedly.

"Well, there is only one thing to do - visit the house

and see. Would you like to join us?" Lady Sarah asked matter-of-factly

"Come with you?" Constable Buckley was not sure what was going on. He had a limited number of experiences dealing with Lady Sarah and her mystery solving.

He did not quite understand why Arwyn took her word as gospel on so many things. He was the junior, and he could say nothing, even though he felt that Constable Evans should have been treated with the respect that he showed to her.

"Have you spoken with Doctor Hales?" Arwyn asked with slight curiosity.

"I do not think that is necessary at this stage," Lady Sarah frowned. "Or is it? Sylvia, what do you think?" Lady Sarah asked.

"I think that we should call on Doctor Hales, and ask the doctor to come with us. It would be useful to have the doctor with us should we discover that something is wrong. If Mr Brown is merely sick in his bed and not called for assistance, the doctor would be the best man to have with us," Sylvia reasoned.

"Quite so. Then Doctor Hales it is. I had hoped to

avoid calling upon him, but I believe you are right," Lady Sarah sighed.

Doctor Hales had taken to fussing over Lady Sarah ever more frequently since the incident at engagement celebrations.

Every time Lady Sarah had seen the doctor in a personal capacity, he had be rather too interested in her well-being, so much so that she was starting to avoid the man.

On the whole, she liked the doctor. But she believed that he was taking his duty of care a little too far and it was interfering with their personal lives at this point.

Arwyn smiled slightly at the tone of voice Lady Sarah used when agreeing to visit the doctor.

"Very well, ladies. In that case, it would be best for you to go without us in attendance. If you do find something of a mystery, do come to me directly. I would hate to be left out of anything," he replied.

Crimes in Stickleback Hollow were often reported to Arwyn, but when something strange was afoot, people always seem to go to Lady Sarah first and, most of the time, the constable was the last to know about those kinds of events taking place in the village.

He knew that Lady Sarah was not doing it out of spite, so it did not irk him. But his professional pride was often hurt when Lady Sarah began an investigation without his input.

Lady Sarah nodded her agreement before the two women departed and Constable Buckley wondered if he would ever understand their dynamic, or where he fitted in the unwritten heirarchy of Stickleback Hollow.

Chapter 2

The ladies turned and made their way to the doctor's house. Richard Hales, the doctor's son and trainee doctor to the village, answered the door.

"Good morning, ladies. The surgery has not started yet, so I am sure you could have sent for my father at the manor," Richard said with a slight frown.

"That is not why we are here, sadly, Richard," Lady Sarah sighed.

"Please come in. I will fetch my father down. He has been slow to rise for the last few days," Richard said, and disappeared back into the house as the two ladies made their way to the sitting room they knew very well. It was a comfortable room, but Lady Sarah was in no mood to relax.

She was becoming rather anxious, and the dismissals of her concern were starting to annoy her, especially when Constable Buckley had done so with such definitive disregard after so short a time in the village.

She was keen to discover what was actually

happening, so the delay in the doctor coming down was yet another frustration on top of everything else.

So rather than sit, she stood by the window, and stared out at the village beyond it. The doctor's house had a pleasant view of the village and of Grangeback Manor.

She could see it, poking its head out of the trees that surrounded it. The great forest that lay between the village and the manor offered privacy from visitors, but also a wonderful view for those who live both at Grangeback and in Stickleback Hollow.

It was a full twenty minutes before the doctor finally appeared, dressed and ready to receive his guests.

"Good morning, ladies. What brings you here at this hour of the day?" the doctor said as he furrowed his brow.

"We are here to ask you to accompany us to. Duffleton Hall," Lady Sarah said.

"You are concerned about Mr Brown?" the doctor asked.

"Indeed," Sylvia said. "No one has seen him for quite some time and her ladyship is worried."

"I see. And have you considered-" the doctor began, but Lady Sarah held up her hand.

"Of course I have considered it. Had I not considered it, every other person in the village asking me if I had considered it, would certainly have made me consider it by now," she said, rather testily.

Richard hid a smirk behind his hand, and glanced at Sylvia. She raised her eyebrows as if to say that she agreed with him.

It was a rarity to see Lady Sarah lose any form of temper, and for her to have lost it so readily with the doctor, it was evident how much his constant fussing over her had irked the lady in the last few months and weeks.

"Very well, if you are this concerned about Mr Brown, let us investigate," the doctor replied.

"I will come along as well," Richard said.

"But the surgery," Doctor Hales began to protest.

"Father, without you here I cannot run the surgery. You need to be on the premises as the qualified physician. I shall simply place a note on the door saying that we will return presently. The afternoon surgery will begin slightly later than normal as a result," Richard said to his father, who nodded.

The doctor seemed to be more fatigued than he

normally was. There was a look in his eye that seemed to suggest that he was ready to begin his retirement, and wishing that his son was ready to take over the duties of his practice.

It was a day that would eventually come, and everyone in the village knew it. To lose someone like Doctor Hales, and to be replaced by his son, was not a prospect they looked forward to.

Jack Hales had taken care of the village for a very long time, and there was a great deal of love for the man in Stickleback Hollow due to the care that he had shown to each and every member of the village.

He was the one that had brought Constable Evans into the fold. The constable was by far the best policeman that the residents had ever seen and they were forever grateful to the doctor for his role in Arwyn's appointment. The doctor had taken care of family members for decades, and there was a great deal of trust in him and his methods.

He did not ignore anything he would consider a warning sign when it came to health, no matter how many times a patient might have been in to see him, or complained of one ailment or another.

Richard Hales was keen to be as good a doctor, if not better than his father was, and to offer the same level of care and devotion to his patients.

Most of the village had known him since he was a boy, and so some of the older members of the community found it hard to see him as anything other than a young boy who had torn around the village, causing trouble with his brother, from a young age.

Those were hardly the actions of a reliable doctor, but over time, he was sure he would win all of them over and create a reputation for himself that was something akin to that of his father.

The four did not walk to Duffleton Hall, but took the doctor's trap. It was a small trap, just big enough for the four of them to travel comfortably, and Richard drove it so that they would get there in a timely manner, especially as his father had taken to becoming a much slower driver over the last few months.

Duffleton Hall was a short jaunt from the village on a good road. It took less than ten minutes on horseback to reach the drive that led up to the manor house.

The walk was somewhat longer, but it was a pleasant

walk, for the most part, but given how tired his father had been recently, and how eager he seemed to be to return to his surgery afterwards, Richard had thought the trap was the best way for them to get there.

As they pulled up the long, gravel driveway, nothing seemed to be amiss at the hall. The building looked just as stoic and strong as it always had.

Lady Sarah and Sylvia both had bad memories of the place from before the property had passed into the hands of Mr Brown.

The house had been vacant since the death of the previous owner, Elizabeth Wessex, who had inherited Duffleton Hall from her fiancé, Mr Daniel Cooper. Both had been murdered, and the building left empty.

It had been purchased by a Doctor Marcus Duckett with rather nefarious motivations, something that both Lady Sarah and Sylvia had fallen afoul of. The rumours had been that he planned to open a sanitorium in the Hall, but a nurse had seemingly hijacked his plans and instead kidnapped fallen women to experiment on.

Lady Sarah and Doctor Hales had been taken by the nurse and her associates from the hospital to the Hall after they had begun to investigate the disappearances of other women from the hospital.

Not only did Lady Sarah and Sylvia meet as captives of the scheming nurse; they had been two amongst hundreds of women that were prisoners because they were believed to be fallen women, steeped in sin, who need to be punished for their crimes against society and God; but it had been in the days following their escape that Lady Sarah had first met Mr Oliver Henry Brown.

She had been in the pit of despair when she had spotted the American walking up to the manor house and it had been his friendship that had saved her from depression and losing herself to her own grief.

Since Mr Brown had taken control of the property, there were better memories to be made, but neither Lady Sarah nor Sylvia had willing been inside the house since Mr Brown had become the owner.

They had not even set foot on the grounds since they had both escaped from the doctor and nurse, but now they were forced to visit the house, both women were focused more on their concern from Mr Brown than the trauma they had suffered.

The trap lurched to a stop outside the front of the house and Doctor Hales quickly alighted. He strode up to the door and knocked firmly upon the giant door using the great bass knocker that decorated it.

The doctor had not thought twice about leaping out of the trap to knock on the door. He was a much harder visitor to turn aside than Lady Sarah was. If Mr Brown did not wish to see her ladyship, that was one thing, but to turn the doctor away was something quite different.

The butler would not be able to dismiss him at the door with instructions that the lord of the manor was not to be disturbed. But it was not the butler who answered the door. Instead it was someone that none of the assembled company had ever seen before.

"Can I help you?" the man at the door asked. His voice was heavily accented in a rather strange way.

"Yes, sir, you can," the doctor replied rather brusquely.

"I see, and how is it that I can help you?" the man asked, seemingly irritated by the doctor's presence.

"I am Doctor Hales, the village physician and I am here to see Mr Brown," the doctor said firmly and made to move past the man at the door and into the house, but the man was prepared for the doctor to try and force his way in.

He blocked the door and forced the doctor to step back.

"Did Mr Brown have an appointment with you, sir?" the man asked lightly.

"He did not. But my charges do not need appointments when I am prepared to make house calls to check on the health of all the residents of this village," the doctor said rather matter-of-factly.

"I see. I am sorry to disappoint you, sir, but Mr Brown is not here at present. Perhaps, to save yourself time, you should consider making appointments with your patients. It will save on pointless journeys," the man said with a smile that didn't reach his eyes.

Lady Sarah stiffened her back as she sat in the trap. There was something about this man she did not like or trust. Richard had not moved from the driver's seat, but he was staring at the house. Not at the man blocking the entrance to the house, but past him, into the hallway where he could see the shadows of three more people loitering inside.

"Where is the butler? It seems rather strange that he is not here to answer a trifling knock at the front door," the doctor replied with a look of suspicion etched on his face.

"He has taken a much deserved holiday," the man replied with a shrug.

"It is equally bizarre that he would not inform us that he was taking a holiday, or that he would indeed take a holiday so soon after taking up his new position," the doctor replied quite frankly.

"I cannot comment on the communication habits of another, I am afraid," the man replied, now eager to see the visitors gone.

"If he has taken a holiday, when might the butler return, and for that matter, when will Mr Brown return?" Doctor Hales asked, his patience now wearing thin.

"Gott im Himmel, I do not know the answer to either question," the man replied curtly, and then cursed himself slightly under his breath.

"I see, and what, sir, is your name?" the doctor asked slowly.

"That is not your concern, doctor. Good day," the man said and slammed the door in the doctor's face.

Lady Sarah sighed, but did not relax. Her hands were folded in her lap but Sylvia could see that she had been digging her fingernails into the palm of her hand in frustration.

Lady Sarah wished she had bought Pattinson with them, but she had not felt it was necessary to bring the dog with her to visit the manor house. Not only that, but Mr Hunter had wanted Pattinson to join him as he walked the estate, hunting foul and game to help control the population of quail and grouse especially.

Though Pattinson was an excellent guard dog, he was most useful at this time of year as a hunting dog. Though a Japanese hunting dog, he was a hunting dog all the same, and his instincts and abilities were something Mr Hunter had come to rely upon.

Though not as adept at chasing rabbits as terriers were, Pattinson was an exceptional retrieval dog and very good at flushing out birds and other game, and large enough to chase off any foxes that might try to come too close to the chickens Cooky kept in her small kitchen garden at Grangeback Manor.

"It seems that your ladyship was quite correct in her

fears after all," Doctor Hales sighed as he returned to the trap and climbed up beside Richard.

"Indeed not," Lady Sarah replied as she chewed her bottom lip.

"What do we do now?" Richard asked, his eyes still fixed on the door to Duffleton Hall.

"We go see Constables vans and Buckley and tell them what we have discovered. It is not much, but there is something most definitely amiss here," Lady Sarah said with resignation.

"And then what will you do?" the doctor asked dryly.

"What do you mean?" Lady Sarah replied as a frown flickered across her face.

"That there is a mystery to be solved here and that since you have arrived in Stickleback Hollow, there has not been a mystery that you could not help but be involved in," Richard said over his shoulder.

"Very well, if anyone was to know if Mr Brown has taken a holiday of some description, then surely his family at Tatton Park would know," Lady Sarah replied thoughtfully.

"That is a fair supposition," Sylvia agreed.

"Very well, that is the next place we shall go," the doctor agreed.

"What of the butler?" Richard asked.

"I think that we need to talk to Wilson as well," Sylvia replied. "He seems to know the comings and goings of all the staff of the great houses in the area, even as far away as Lyme Park."

"Then we shall speak with him as well," the doctor said and Richard flicked the reins, lurching the trap into motion.

From inside Duffleton Hall, four sets of eyes watched them depart.

Chapter 3

Lady Sarah was relieved to be away from Duffleton Hall. She was of the opinion that nothing good could come from that building and that it must surely be cursed. The first resident she had known to live in the Hall was Mr Henry Cartwright, a reformed criminal, whose son had tried to kill Lady Sarah when she had first arrived in Stickleback Hollow.

He had lost the Hall due to poor financial decisions, and it had then laid empty until Mr Daniel Cooper had bought it. The first of Mr Hunter's rivals for Lady Sarah's affection, his murder had seen the Hall pass to his eventual fiancée, Miss Elizabeth Wessex. When she in turn had been killed, the Hall had remained empty until the doctor and nurse that had kidnapped Lady Sarah began to use it for their experiments.

Now Mr Oliver Henry Brown had disappeared from the Hall, and Lady Sarah was certain that it would be far better if the building was torn down and turned into a pile of rubble.

Her stomach was tied up in knots with worry and she was certain that her friend was in great danger. Richard and Doctor Hales didn't speak a word as Richard drove the trap back down to the village. He pushed the horses to the fastest trot he could without risking the safety to the passengers, and took turns a little too sharply for his father's liking.

Sylvia sat beside Lady Sarah and watched her mistress with concern. She knew that Lady Sarah held a great deal of love for Mr Brown, and in her mind, she believe that Mr Brown was a much better match for Lady Sarah than Mr Hunter would ever be.

Sylvia believed that Lady Sarah's aversion to Duffleton Hall was part of the reason she had chosen Mr Hunter over her American suitor, and that had the gentleman known the history that the Estate had, and how Lady Sarah felt about it, he would have found a different home in the neighbourhood to purchase.

It took far less time to return to the village with Richard's driving verging on reckless. Constable Evans and Constable Buckley were both still in the police house, neither had expected Lady Sarah to return that day, so when the doctor's trap arrived in a hurry, with the four occupants aboard, the two policemen were at a loss as to why they had arrived in such a state.

"Are you aware that Mr Brown's home has guests in his home, but both he and his butler have mysteriously left the village without a word to anyone?" the doctor asked as he pushed open the door to the police house. He did not offer any form of greeting to the two men, nor did he feel that there was any need to observe any formalities.

"Both the butler and Mr Brown are missing?" Arwyn frowned as Richard, Sylvia, and Lady Sarah followed the doctor into the police house.

"They are," Richard said seriously.

"Are they missing or are they simply absent from the Hall?" Constable Buckley mused.

"Ultimately, does it not amount to the same thing?" Sylvia said with a raised eyebrow.

"Perhaps, but if they are truly missing then we have grounds to act, if they are simply absent from the Hall, that may be somewhat harder for us to intervene in," Thompson shrugged.

"That is why I am going to ask you not to look for them," Lady Sarah replied.

"Not to find them?" Arywn asked with confusion.

"Indeed. Instead, I want you to watch the Hall and the occupants within it. We do not know why they are there or what they are doing. We do not know if the rest of the household staff is safe, or whether Mr Brown and his butler are captives within its walls. We cannot storm the Hall, so I would have you watch to see what you can learn," Lady Sarah explained.

"I see, and what will you do whilst we are watching the Hall?" Constable Evans asked thoughtfully.

"We shall begin by visiting Wilson's Inn to inquire about the butler. Wilson or Emma will surely have heard if he were planning a trip or had to leave the Hall for some reason. Then we shall go to Tatton Park to speak with the Egertons about Mr Brown," Lady Sarah said.

"Very well, we should take the watch on the Hall in shifts, then there is always someone here at the police house," Constable Buckley suggested.

"I think that we should send to Chester for assistance. Constables McIntyre and Cantello could be here in a matter of hours. With two men already missing, I am not sure we should be watching the Hall alone," Constable Evans said as he swung his cape about his shoulders and prepared to head out to investigate the Hall for himself.

"Very well, I shall go to Chester on your behalf in the trap. Write whatever you need to request the help," the doctor sighed and glanced at his pocketwatch.

"I will go back to the surgery and help those with minor ailments and prepare a list of people for you to visit this afternoon, father," Richard assured him and the doctor nodded his thanks.

"Very well, we shall meet at Grangeback this evening to discuss what we have learned," Lady Sarah instructed, and with Sylvia beside her, set out in the direction of Wilson's Inn.

Wilson's Inn was the social hub of the village. There was nothing that happened in Stickleback Hollow, or the surrounding area, that was a secret in the village pub. The staff from the great houses in the neighbourhood spent their time off in the inn, the labourers, the farmers, the shopkeepers, and even the aristocracy. The social diversity was something truly special to behold, and as a result, if the butler at Duffleton Hall had taken an impromptu holiday, Wilson would know.

The inn was run by Wilson, and his wife, Emma. Wilson handled the drinks and the patrons, whilst Emma cooked all the meals and took care of the rooms. Her cooking was famed throughout the county, being second only to the fine culinary creations of Cooky at Grangeback Manor.

The inn was a short walk from the police house and neither Lady Sarah nor Sylvia minded the walk. Richard was bound in the opposite direction to the two women, and they heard the doctor departing not long after they did.

Lady Sarah knew it would take the two policemen sometime to make the necessary preparation before they departed for Duffleton Hall, and there was nothing that could be gained from lamenting the Hall remaining unwatched for the moment. Things had been set in motion and that would have to suffice for now.

Instead, she focused her mind on the questions she would ask at the inn. As she walked, Lady Sarah realised that she wasn't even sure of what the name of the butler was. The staff at Duffleton Hall were all hired by Mr Brown after he bought the property, though he had asked Bosworth and the butler at Tatton Park for advice on who would be appropriate to take up the vacant positions in the household.

Sylvia was equally ignorant of who the staff at Duffleton Hall were. Though she was employed by Lady Sarah, she was not on the same social level as those who worked in service at the great houses in the neighbourhood, and so was excluded from the gossip circles and camaraderie that existed in the downstairs world.

She was stuck between the upstairs and the downstairs, and though the family at Grangeback treated her as though she was part of it, those in wider society were far less welcoming to her.

The inn was not busy when the two ladies stepped in out of the rather warm summer's day. The fire grate was empty as there was no need to heat the room with such a fierce heat outside. However the relative heat of August had not done much to help with the flooding that threatened the village. May and June had been unseasonably wet and the whole country had seen flooding as the summer had continued.

The village had been mostly spared, but the threat of the lake and rivers that ran through both the estates of Grangeback and Duffleton Hall had many constantly worrying about Stickleback Hollow becoming a new Venice.

The threat of flooding was another reason that Lady Sarah thought it so strange that both Mr Oliver Henry Brown and his butler would both just disappear without warning.

Wilson was stood behind the bar cleaning glasses and they could hear Emma banging away with her pots and pans in the kitchen. It would not be long before the lunches would be taken out to those who worked on some of the farms and on the land around the village.

There was a standing arrangement with the land owners that Emma would provide lunches for them at no cost to the recipients. The brigadier had explained it was part of noblesse oblige, the responsibility of those who owned the great houses of England to not only protect and safeguard the properties and land, but the people that worked for them. Most of the workers lived in tithed cottages on the land they worked, earned enough to feed and clothe their families and could gather as much firewood as they needed from the forests on the land without chopping down any of the trees.

The lunches were something extra, and not only did it help to sustain the small village inn, but it meant that workers who came to the lands around Stickleback Hollow rarely moved on looking for greener pastures.

"Good morning, your ladyship, Sylvia. Not often we see you at this time of day. What can we do for you?" Wilson asked brightly, with a slight hint of confusion in his eyes.

"Good morning, Wilson," Lady Sarah replied, but her voice was lacking the same light tone that Wilson's had.

"We've come to ask you about the butler at Duffleton Hall, if you don't mind," Sylvia said as she glanced about the room.

She wanted to make sure the butler was not hiding in a dark corner of the inn. It was unlikely that he would be there, but the lady's companion wanted to be certain.

"The butler? Do you mean Forestque?" Wilson asked with a slight smile. "He wouldn't call himself a butler, but Mr Brown hired him for the position in Duffleton Hall anyway."

There was a laughter in Wilson's voice which

confused Sylvia and Lady Sarah.

"What is so amusing?" Sylvia frowned.

"I take it that you haven't been introduced into Fortesque yet?" Wilson replied kindly. "He's something of an acquired taste, but fitting for an American trying to fit into the upper echelons of society."

Lady Sarah smiled to herself and shook her head.

"Fitting? I see," she said slowly.

"What is it that you wanted to know about him?" Wilson asked lightly. "He's not offended anyone, has he?"

"No, nothing like that," Sylvia said firmly.

"When did you last see him?" Lady Sarah asked innocently.

"It's been a few days, my lady. I expected him to be in last night. But he didn't come down from the Hall, no one from Duffleton has been in for at least three nights now," Wilson said, as though he had not thought it was strange until that very moment.

"Then he did not mention a holiday of any kind when you last saw him?" Sylvia sighed and shook her head.

"No, none, and he's not the sort to take a holiday, if you follow my meaning," Wilson said. "Work is his life and if he stopped working, well he might as well be dead. A tipple of an evening off is as close to a holiday as a man like Fortesque will ever get."

"Much like yourself then?" Lady Sarah grinned at the barkeep.

"It's how I recognise the type, my lady," Wilson replied with good humour. "Is he alright? No one from the Hall visiting and now your questions, has something happened?"

"We don't know, but it is possible that he is in some trouble," Lady Sarah sighed as the door to the inn opened.

"Trouble? Then you weren't wrong?" Mr Hunter asked as he and the two Baker boys stepped through the doorway.

The tall son of the brigadier had only heard the end of the conversation, but he knew all too well that if there was any mystery or danger to stumble across, his fiancée would find it before anyone else.

"Never known her ladyship to be wrong about anything," Wilson frowned and stroked his chin. "Maybe you should all sit down and I'll fetch some lunch for you. Then, if your ladyship would be so kind, you'd tell me what's happened to Fortesque - or at least what you think has happened."

Lady Sarah nodded her agreement and made her way over to one of the vacant tables as Wilson ducked into the kitchen to have Emma prepare the group some lunch.

Sylvia sat down and looked at Mr Hunter with a steady, hard stare that she reserved for situations where she wanted certain parties to understand that apologies were owed to her mistress and she would not be satisfied until they were made.

"Where is Pattinson?" Lady Sarah asked, hoping he was waiting outside the inn, enjoying the sunshine.

"Back at the manor. He was a little tired after all his exercise this morning," Mr Hunter shrugged. "Mrs Bosworth and Cooky refused to let him leave again once we took them the birds."

Lady Sarah made no further comment and the group lapsed into a rather uncomfortable silence.

It took almost no time for Wilson to bring out a tray of soup with wedges of bread and butter for lunch for the party, and it was eaten gratefully. Soup was not a normal dish to serve given the time of year, but it was something easy for Emma to have cooking for any guests at the inn whilst she prepared the lunches for the workers in the fields.

"Now then, what is there to know about Fortesque and Mr Brown?" Wilson said as he sat down with his guests as they ate.

Emma could be heard bustling around in the kitchen, but showed no signs of coming out to join them.

"They are both missing," Sylvia said quite matter-of-factly, still staring accusingly at Mr Hunter.

"Both of them? Then perhaps they have gone somewhere together," Mr Hunter offered with a slight shrug.

"That's hardly likely," Wilson frowned.

"What makes you say that?" Mr Hunter asked, trying not to sound irritated about being contradicted by the innkeeper.

"Fortesque isn't that kind of butler. He's got some very strange peculiarities that make him unlikely to go anywhere alone with Mr Brown, let alone go on such a journey without informing anyone else," Wilson replied thoughtfully.

"Not only have the pair gone missing, but there are some suspicious individuals that have taken up residence in

Duffleton Hall," Lady Sarah said slowly.

"Suspicious individuals?" Stanley asked as he sat bolt upright. He glanced at his brother, who had the same reaction to the news.

"They refused the doctor entry to the house. No servants came to the door and only strangers that spoke in a foreign language seemed to be in the house," Sylvia replied.

"Only one of them spoke with the doctor, but there were shadows of others just inside the door," Lady Sarah sighed and shook her head.

"They claimed that the butler had gone on holiday and that Mr Brown was not at home," Sylvia said tartly. "And when the doctor pressed to enter the house, he was refused. The constables are surveilling the Hall now."

"Then Mr Brown and Fortesque are truly missing?" Mr Hunter frowned.

"That is what we intend to discover. My biggest fear is that they are not missing but hostages within the Hall," Lady Sarah said with a heavy sigh. "But I also wish to be certain that Mr Brown has not gone somewhere of his own volition."

"And how do you intend to do that?" Mr Hunter

asked as he leaned back in his chair.

"Once we were certain that Fortesque had not informed anyone here of a planned holiday or sudden departure, we were to go to Tatton Park to speak with the Egertons. If Mr Brown has left to give himself some space from life here in Stickleback Hollow, he would almost certainly have told at least one of the Egertons," Lady Sarah said calmly, though her patience with her fiancé was starting to wear thin.

"You are going to Tatton Park?" Lee asked.

"That is the intention," Sylvia grinned at the young man.

"Then can we come too?" Stanley said urgently.

"Of course, I am sure that Charlotte and Charles will be pleased to see you both," Lady Sarah replied kindly.

"In that case, I will stay here and attempt to find out what is happening inside the Hall," Mr Hunter sighed.

"How do you intend to do that?" Sylvia asked archly.

"By entering the Hall through the servants' entrance and exploring," Mr Hunter shrugged.

"A man of your size is not built for stealth," Sylvia said dryly.

"Perhaps not, but I can hunt without being seen by deer and game birds on the estate. Searching the Hall will not be all that different," Mr Hunter said through slightly gritted teeth.

"Very well, Lee and Stanley shall accompany us to Tatton Park. Perhaps the doctor and Richard will wish to join us, as long as they do not have too many patients to attend to," Lady Sarah said, doing her best to stop an argument breaking out between Mr Hunter and Sylvia.

"I will keep my ears open for any news here. We won't see our regular customers for a few hours yet, but when we do, we'll see what we can learn for you," Wilson said as he slapped his hand on the table.

He seemed rather excited by the prospect of being involved in one of the famed investigations of Lady Sarah. Many had taken place in the village, but Wilson, for the most part, had very little to do with them.

This was the first occasion he felt that he could truly contribute to helping solve a mystery and was already planning how he would retell the tale to those patrons who were just passing through the village.

"Very well, come boys, Sylvia, we should not delay,"

Lady Sarah said firmly as she rose from the table. "Thank Emma for the soup, as well, please, Wilson."

"I shall. She'll be glad to hear you enjoyed it, my lady," Wilson said, tugging at his forelock as he moved to clear the table.

Chapter 4

The doctor and Richard were only too glad to leave the confines of the doctor's rooms. There had only been one patient all morning that had needed attention and no calls for the doctor to attend anyone at home.

There was always the risk that leaving the village without a doctor for a few hours would be tempting fate, but Jack Hales was not a man that had ever let anything as fickle as destiny govern his actions.

Richard drove the six companions to Tatton Park in the doctor's trap. It was a tight squeeze, but it was not a long journey to the great house.

The senior Egertons were not at home, having traveled to London the previous morning upon the business of Parliament. The ladies had all gone too, save for young Charlotte, to visit the shops that London had to offer and bring back some of the latest styles to northern realms ahead of Lady Sarah's upcoming wedding.

The entire Egerton clan had been invited to the festivities, and some other important personages were expected to also attend. As such an illustrious list of personages were expected, the Egerton ladies had no intention of being seen in unfashionable clothing.

Thomas and Edward were both at home, along with the young twins, Charles and Charlotte.

"My dear Lady Sarah, what an unexpected pleasure!" Thomas said brightly as the party was shown into the summer parlour.

"I wish that it was pleasure that brought us here," Lady Sarah sighed as she was greeted by the two older Egerton brothers and invited to sit.

"I see," Edward said as a frown flickered across his face.

"Where are Charlotte and Charles?" Lee asked as he glanced about the parlour.

"Somewhere upstairs I think," Thomas said with a wave of his hand. "Feel free to try and find them. Only, don't upset the housekeeper."

Lee and Stanley both nodded earnestly and then dashed from the room as fast as their legs could carry them.

Edward moved across the parlour and pulled the bell cord. The butler appeared a few moments later, and Edward said something quietly to him before the butler nodded and left the room, silently closing the door behind him.

"Now, what is it that brings you here?" Thomas said as the six adults sat down to talk.

"Your cousin," Lady Sarah said as she shifted slightly uncomfortably on the sofa she was sat on. Sylvia was beside her and Richard was beside the lady's companion.

The doctor sat in an armchair a good distance away from everyone else, close to the fireplace. There was no fire lit as the weather did not call for the room to be heated, but there was a slight draft that came from the flu that the doctor found preferable to the stuffiness the summer weather often afforded.

"I see, are you still worried about him not visiting?" Edward asked with slight amusement.

"I see that someone has been gossiping," Sylvia said under her breath.

"You, of all people, should know that gossip between great houses spreads faster than any plague," Thomas replied dryly.

"I am worried because there are strangers at Duffleton Hall, who answer the door instead of the butler, and deny people entry," the doctor piped up gruffly.

"Strangers? Fortesque would never allow anyone else to answer the door at the Hall, unless he is dead or force to leave for some reason," Edward frowned.

"Both your cousin and his man seem to be missing," Richard said flatly. "The butler has not left the area, at least not willingly, as far as we can tell."

"We came to ask whether Mr Brown had told you he was taking a vacation of some description, a tour of the lakes perhaps to clear his head," Lady Sarah said calmly. She knew that Richard was becoming more agitated simply because Sylvia was growing more so. Her lady's maid was fiercely loyal and was starting to take the doubts about Lady Sarah's concerns very personally.

"He has not, at least he has not confined as much in any of the family," Thomas replied. He glanced at his brother, who shook his head.

"That does not strike you as strange then? That he would not inform you he was departing?" Sylvia asked with her eyebrow raised.

"If he had decided to take a holiday somewhere, it is most out of character for him to inform no one, and I agree that Fortesque not answering the door and allowing strangers to do so is also very odd," Edward said slowly.

"To be honest with you, we haven't seen or heard from Oliver since your engagement and all the business that went along with the festivities," Thomas said delicately. There was no need to bring up the attempt on Lady Sarah's life when all present were very aware of what had transpired.

"And you did not find this unusual?" the doctor barked.

"No, well at least not for a man that was heartbroken and somewhat jilted," Thomas replied without thinking.

"He was not jilted," Sylvia snapped harshly.

"Forgive me, I do not begrudge Hunter his good fortune in securing the favour of her ladyship, but for a man that has loved her and done nothing but support her and care for her, it could easily be seen as being jilted," Thomas said firmly.

"Unrequited love is just that. No woman is under any obligation to return a gentleman's feelings," Richard sighed heavily, with a sideways glance at Sylvia.

"Quite, but this is not the discussion we should be having at present," Edward said sternly. He could see how increasingly uncomfortable Lady Sarah was becoming and wanted to shift the conversation back to the disappearances rather than the cause.

"Quite," the doctor agreed. "So Mr Brown has been somewhat anti-social since the engagement party?"

"He has," Edward confirmed. "Ordinarily we would visit or hear from him a few times a week, but we have had nothing."

"And this was not considered to be strange?" Richard frowned.

"As I said, we assumed that he was brooding and did not want to be disturbed. Somewhat understandably," Thomas said archly.

"Thank you, both, that does help," Lady Sarah said quietly.

"Your ladyship, we did not mean any offence or to imply that you were-" Thomas began but Lady Sarah held up her hand to silence him.

"Please, we have more important things to worry

about," she said in an even voice, doing her best to not betray her own emotions.

"Perhaps we should attempt to visit and see these strangers for ourselves," Edward volunteered.

"It could possibly do some good, at least it is harder for strangers to deny family access to the Hall," the doctor said, rubbing his chin thoughtfully.

"I agree, if you are not opposed to the task. At the very least it might serve to draw out these strangers and allow our dear policemen to be able to help in an official capacity," Lady Sarah replied.

"You think there may be some form of public disorder?" Thomas asked with a grin.

"No, they seem to practiced at civility to be goaded into violence, at least in the open. Seeing just how many there are and if you the physically try to bar you from the house, that will be all the evidence we need that they are occupying the Hall without Mr Brown's consent," Lady Sarah replied.

"Then Charlotte and Charles should join us. They are rather adept at slipping into places they should not be - especially if someone is trying to prevent them from entering somewhere," Edward grinned.

As if to punctuate the point, a large crash sounded from the floors above and the voice of the housekeeper, yelling at the top of her lungs rang out.

"I think now would be a good time to retrieve the Baker boys and see what Hunter has managed to learn from his own reconnaissance," Richard said dryly and the others agreed.

Chapter 5

The best time to infiltrate any building is when intruders are not expected, at least as far as Mr Hunter was concerned. However, this was generally during hours of darkness and not when the entire household would be awake and working.

Mr Hunter as not prepared to wait until the night set in to try to enter the Hall undetected. He was still almost certain that Lady Sarah was overreacting,and there was nothing suspicious about Mr Brown having some foreign guests.

If he was found wandering the Hall, he was known in the village and it could easily be explained away, especially given how many of the staff at the Hall would have seen him at Wilson's Inn.

The cook at Duffleton Hall had been recommended to the position by Cooky, and Mr Hunter had met her on a few occasions. Her name was Muriel and she was a friendly woman, quiet but friendly. She was not quite the busty and bustling figure that Cooky was, but she was good at her job and took a great deal of pride in her cooking.

She had been married young, but sadly widowed and had used her skills in the kitchen to help her deal with the passing of her husband.

Mr Hunter decided that rather than trying to snoop around the hallways, he would call on Muriel at the backdoor and see what he could learn from her.

Duffleton Hall, like Grangeback Manor, had a kitchen door that lead to a garden where some seasonal vegetables and herbs were grown for use in the house. Duffleton Hall did not have the chicken coop that Grangeback Manor had, but the two buildings had been designed by the same architect, so their layout was not dissimilar.

Mr Hunter made his way around the edge of the Hall's land and then cut across in the direction of the kitchen. He was sure that the policemen would not see him as they would be watching the front of the property rather than the trade entrance.

He opened the gate to the kitchen garden quietly and approached the door, making sure to glance through the window first to make sure Muriel was alone.

He tapped quietly on the glass when he saw her, and watched the poor woman jump at the sound. He frowned and felt his heart sinking in his chest.

Muriel might be a quiet woman, but she was steady and not one to be easily frightened - especially by a tap on the window or door during daylight hours.

She glanced about furtively before opening the door to Mr Hunter.

"Mr Hunter, I am afraid now is not a good time to call upon us," Muriel hissed as she kept one eye over her shoulder.

"That is precisely why I am here, Muriel," Mr Hunter replied in a low voice.

"Then you know what has happened to the Master and Fortesque?" she asked, her normal demeanour replaced with pleading eyes and a desperate tone to her voice.

"No, I am afraid I do not. But their absence has been noticed, and not just by me," Mr Hunter assured her. "Can you tell me all you know about what happened before they disappeared?"

"I will try. The routine in the Hall has been disrupted somewhat recently. The new housekeeper is rather set in her ways, which has meant a lot of things changed. She and Fortesque do not get on well, and it's caused a bit of fracture. The Master needs a good housekeeper, but I don't want to speak out of turn," Muriel said, her voice low and fear was clearly creeping into it.

"There is no speaking out of turn. Simply tell me what you remember," Mr Hunter said gently.

"Well Fortesque and Mrs Hubbard, that's the housekeeper, had been clashing you might say. Mr Brown had been good about soothing them both and finding a compromise for them both to live with, but when her ladyship turned down his proposal of marriage; well the Master stopped trying to help them get along," Muriel explained.

"It's rare for a master of a house to go that far to ensure harmony amongst his staff without removing one of them from their position," Mr Hunter said, almost to himself.

"Oh the Master is very good. He always things about us and making our lives here good. I've never known a Master like him. I am ever so grateful to Cooky, but it's why I am so worried, you see," Muriel said quickly.

"I understand, please continue," Mr Hunter urged her.

"Well when his proposal was rejected, he took to his bed chamber and didn't want to leave it. He made a good showing at your engagement party, but when her ladyship's life was in danger, he was even more worried. After all that happened, Fortesque was quite insistent that the Master should go away for a while, go see some other part of England for a while," Muriel said.

"It is often a good way to soothe the soul," Mr Hunter said with a slight shake of his head. He had left Stickleback Hollow on two occasions in order to clear his own head. The second time had been more akin to running away from his problems in a rather selfish way - something Mrs Bosworth had never let him forget.

"Mr Brown didn't want to go, but then one morning, he was gone. Mrs Hubbard said he wasn't in his rooms and then Fortesque was missing too. Nobody had seen either of them leave, but Mrs Hubbard was sure they were together, wherever they were, and that we should carry on as normal. Then the strangers came to the house. They had a letter from the Master and well-" Muriel paused as she thought better of saying the next part of the sentence.

"Well?" Mr Hunter asked.

"Oh please, sir. I don't want to speak out of turn," Muriel begged him.

"You are not speaking out of turn, what is it?" Mr Hunter said gently.

"Well, she seemed to know the strangers. One of the maids heard her talking some foreign language with them one evening when everyone was supposed to be in bed," Muriel said.

"I see," Mr Hunter said thoughtfully.

"Mr Hunter, please tell me, is the Master in danger?" Muriel asked nervously.

"I do not know," Mr Hunter admitted. "But I do know that her ladyship will not rest until we know not only where Mr Brown is, but that he is safe as well."

Muriel nodded her head a little sadly.

"You should go, Mr Hunter, before Mrs Hubbard comes," Muriel said urgently.

"I will, but before I do, will you do something for me?" Mr Hunter asked.

"What is it, sir?" Muriel asked as she glanced about

as though she feared Mrs Hubbard could appear from nowhere at any given moment.

"If there are any maids you can trust to not report to Mrs Hubbard, have them listen at any keyholes they can. It's not proper, I know, but if we are to find out why the strangers are here and what has happened to our friends, the more information we have, the better. I will come back, until then, keep yourself safe," Mr Hunter said and patted Muriel on the shoulder as comfortingly as he could.

Muriel watched him leave the garden, almost silently and was glad that the tall man was far more stealthy than his height would suggest. She worried for a moment that he would be seen, but all of the rooms at the back of the house belonged to the staff and everyone would be working.

She stepped out into the garden for a moment and clipped some sage and rosemary to use in the evening meal, and then went to check on the progress of some of the vegetables that would soon be ready for harvest.

It was a small thing, but enough to explain away the door to the garden being open for so long should there be anyone who noticed the draft and wondered what the cook was doing.

She sighed to herself as she moved between the garden beds and felt a slight sense of relief that the people of Stickleback Hollow cared about those at the Hall, at least enough to notice when something was wrong. It was not like that everywhere, and though some might consider it intrusive, it was definitely better than the alternative.

Chapter 6

Lady Sarah did not speak as the trap was driven back from Tatton Park. Far from assuaging her fears, the visit had only compounded them.

Not only had none of the Egertons heard from Mr Brown, it was clear that at least Thomas blamed her for the pain that Mr Brown was enduring. She knew that she should have rejected the proposals of both Mr Brown and Mr Hunter when they both made them to her. She could have explained the need for time and the need for her to understand her own mind before she could possibly consider any proposals, but instead she had kept both men hanging on for months whilst she went back and forth between them and who her future lay with.

There were times she was not certain she had made the right choice, but she had followed her heart and done what was best for her. That was all she could do, even if it did hurt someone else around her.

But now it was far worse than simply hurting

someone else emotionally. She was certain that had she declined Mr Brown's proposal when it was first made then he would not have been vulnerable to these strangers and whatever fate they had in store for him.

His sudden disappearance would not have been so easily dismissed as a man hiding away from the pain of losing a woman to another man.

Her concerns would not have been so readily dismissed by those around her because they were all so certain of the reason for his lack of presence in the village.

But what now worried her more than anything else was where he was. No one had seen him leave the village, the idea that he had taken a holiday without informing any of his family was ridiculous.

So that left only one possible conclusion - Mr Brown was being held against his will somewhere. She did not know whether that was in Duffleton Hall or if the strangers had managed to smuggle him out of the house and to some other location where he could be held and not discovered by the servants, but either way, he was a prisoner and needed to be rescued.

Richard drove the trap back to Grangeback Manor

and left his friends and father at the manor before he went back to the doctor's surgery to see whether there had been any patients that required their attention whilst they had been to Tatton Park.

Brigadier George Webb-Kneelingroach was sat in his study with his son, Mr Hunter, and Pattinson was sleeping by the empty fireplace. The two were sipping on large glasses of whisky and both wore rather somber expressions when Mrs Bosworth came to inform them of Lady Sarah's return.

The brigadier rose slowly from his chair and led Alexander out of the study to the library, where Lady Sarah liked to spend her time.

Pattinson raced ahead of the pair to greet his mistress and was met with an absent-minded pat on the head.

"Dear Sarah, you are owed the most sincere apology I can muster," the brigadier said as he entered the room.

"Oh?" Sylvia asked with a rather unamused expression on her face. Though she was a servant in the household, she was not one to keep her opinions to herself, and the brigadier often welcomed her bluntness.

"Yes, we both must apologise," Mr Hunter admitted.

"Then you were able to discover some things at the Hall?" the doctor asked as he sat down in one of the high-backed chairs.

"I spoke with the cook. She had a great deal to say about what has been happening there. But one thing is certain, Mr Brown is not simply off licking his wounds in private. I fear that not only is he in danger, but all those in his household are. Though, perhaps not the housekeeper," Mr Hunter explained.

Sylvia waited for him to continue, but when it was clear that Mr Hunter had finished, she arched her eyebrow and said,

"There was still not apology."

Mr Hunter frowned at her but the brigadier nodded.

"Quite so, Sylvia, quite so. Sarah, I apologise for so readily dismissing your concerns. I apologise for not trusting your instincts and for trivialising your concerns. You deserved better consideration than you have been afforded and I shall never doubt you in such a fashion again," the brigadier said with heartfelt sincerity.

"Thank you," Lady Sarah said. "Your apology is accepted and you are forgiven."

"I also, apologise," Mr Hunter said, bowing slightly. He would not say more in front of others, but when he had a moment alone with his fiancée, he would make sure he apologised properly.

"Thank you," Lady Sarah replied, knowing that a proper apology would come later.

"Then what do we do now?" the doctor asked with a heavy sigh.

"There is only one thing that can be done. Whilst Edward and Thomas attempt to gain entrance to Duffleton Hall through the front door, Mr Hunter and the Baker boys must infiltrate the Hall through the kitchen and explore the Hall. No one has seen Mr Brown or Fortesque leaving the Estate or Stickleback Hollow. That means that they are either being held in the Hall or they have been taken elsewhere to be imprisoned," Lady Sarah reasoned.

"Which means that if they are in the Hall, then at the very least, Mrs Hubbard will know where they are," Mr Hunter said thoughtfully.

"And if they are not in the Hall, there may be information about where they are now, or one of the servants may have seen something they do not know they saw," Sylvia finished the thought.

"Do you think the Egertons will provide enough of a distraction whilst they search?" the brigadier asked with concern.

"If Charlotte and Charles are with them, I think they could cause enough distraction for an elephant to be lead through the house without them noticing," Lady Sarah smiled in spite of herself.

"Very well, we'll leave at once. Come Lee, Stanley," Mr Hunter said firmly and the two Baker boys eagerly followed him from the room.

"And what do we do in the meantime?" the doctor asked.

"We sit and wait. There is nothing more we can do for the moment. It may not seem to be the most proactive thing that we can do, but without information, there is nothing else we can do," Lady Sarah said slowly.

"My dear Sarah, please try not to fret," the brigadier said gently.

"I cannot help but worry," Lady Sarah sighed. "We all know that when people are kidnapped or held against their will, there is only so much time that those individuals are useful. And when they are no longer useful-" her voice trailed off.

Everyone present knew that Lady Sarah was thinking about what happen to Grace and that her fears were being amplified by the death of her previous companion.

They had been so close to rescuing her when she had been killed for helping Mr Hunter escape from the men that had held her and Millie prisoner for such a long time.

Lady Sarah had searched for months, unsuccessfully, to find the pair after they had been kidnapped, and she refused to let the disappearance of Mr Brown turn out the same way that their quest to find Grace and Millie had.

"I am sure that we shall find them both and soon," Sylvia said kindly, but though Lady Sarah gave her a weak smile and nodded, it was clear that she would not relax until Mr Brown and Fortesque were both safe and they knew who exactly the strangers were that had taken up residence in Duffleton Hall.

Chapter 7

The Egertons did not know that Mr Hunter and the Baker boys planned to infiltrate the Hall whilst they attempted to gain access, but they did want to put on a the biggest spectacle they could, in order to draw out these strangers for the benefit of the policemen, with the intention of provoking a violent reaction that would allow for them to be arrested.

They had chosen the largest carriage that the family possessed to carry them from Tatton Park to Duffleton Hall. It was so large that it had to be pulled by a team of eight grey Hanoverians and would not look out of place in a royal procession.

Two drivers were required for the carriage and Thomas had decided to bring four footmen along to help with creating an air of prestige as they arrived.

Mr Hunter watched the carriage pulling up the long driveway from the treeline and smiled to himself. The policemen had not been warned of their arrival and he dearly wished he could see Arwyn's reaction at that moment. But he had a more pressing task ahead of him.

He watched as two of the footmen leapt off the back of the carriage and rushed round to help the Egertons alight, whilst the other two footman walk up to the front door to announce them.

He smiled to himself and was certain that whatever unfolded at the front of the house would certainly give him time to find whatever he could in the Hall to help them at least discover what had become of Mr Brown.

With Stanley and Lee beside him, Mr Hunter led the way through the treeline, careful to stay just out of sight of all the windows. He didn't think that any of the strangers would be looking out at the gardens and beyond, but he wasn't sure about the housekeeper.

The three made their way to the kitchen door at the back of the house and found Muriel working hard to prepare the evening meal. She didn't have any maids to help her or footmen, which struck Mr Hunter as odd.

In a house of the size of Duffleton Hall, Mr Hunter would have expected there to be at least scullery three maids to help the cook in the kitchen. At Grangeback, Cooky had four kitchen boys and eight scullery maids to help her and often complained that there were not enough hands to get all of the work done.

Though it was strange, Mr Hunter did not have to time to worry about why the house was so woefully understaffed now. He tapped on the door and Muriel almost jumped out of her skin.

She hurried to the back door and opened it with a look of fear on her face.

"Mr Hunter, why are you back here so soon?" she hissed under her breath.

"Don't fret, Muriel, I said I would be back," Mr Hunter smiled reassuringly at the frightened cook.

"But you can't be. There's such a commotion at the front door. The Master's family are here and arguing with the strangers about coming in. Mrs Hubbard will be here at any moment to refuse them entry and if she sees you-" Muriel said with genuine fear.

"Peace, Muriel, peace. We shall not be found. We will be quick and quiet, but we have to search to see if we can find Fortesque and Mr Brown. Our friends will provide a great distraction, and should Charles and Charlotte manage to break through the barricades, help them however you can," Mr Hunter said warmly.

The kitchen at Duffleton Hall was at the back of the house with only the dining room lying between it and the entrance hall. To either side of the kitchen were the long sweeping corridors that ran around the Hall with staircases to each of the upper floors of each wing.

"Lee, Stanley, you know what to do. Stay out of sight and be quick," Mr Hunter said to the two Baker boys. The pair nodded and dashed off through the left hand door of the kitchen.

The sounds coming from the front of the Hall were muted by the closed door between the kitchen and dining room, but Mr Hunter could still make out Thomas and Edward's voices. They were both raised and clearly the two men were close to losing their respective tempers.

Mr Hunter couldn't be sure what Charles and Charlotte were doing, but he had no doubt that they would keep Mrs Hubbard more than occupied whilst the house was searched.

There was a second door that led off from the kitchen

to the opposite wing to the one the Baker boys had gone to explore, and it was this door that Mr Hunter went towards.

"Please, be careful," Muriel begged as she watched Mr Hunter leave the kitchen and tried to block out the noises coming from beyond the dining room.

"Don't worry, we'll get to the bottom of this," Mr Hunter assured her before he slipped through the door.

There were no dogs at Duffleton Hall, and Mr Hunter had begun to believe that they were an essential part of life at a manor house. Not just for the practical aspects of hunting and for companionship, but for situations like this.

He had lost count of the number of times that Pattinson had protected Lady Sarah or helped find someone who had gone missing. There were hounds that had been gifted to Sylvia as well that were being raised and trained to not only hunt but protect the family too.

He was certain that when Mr Brown returned, Lady Sarah would insist that the man get at least one dog. It would be light for a number of hours still, but the overcast sky meant that the hallways of the manor house were rather dim and none of the lamps had been lit.

He made his way down the corridor and tried each

of the rooms in turn, first listening at the door for any signs of life within. None of the ground floor rooms had been disturbed, in fact, Mr Hunter was certain that it had been weeks since anyone had been in them at all.

As he reached the final room before the entrance hall, he could hear shouts from the front door in foreign voices and knew that Charles and Charlotte had dashed into the house. He ducked quickly into the room he was about to investigate and closed the door as the sound of young feet running pounded past the door.

He found himself in the music room and knew he would have to wait a few moments for things to settle down before he could continue exploring the house. There were still the upper floors to investigate and the only way to them was via the two rear staircases or the staircase in the entrance hall.

From the angry voices, now shouting back and forth at one another, it was painfully clear he would be unable to use the entrance hall staircase, but then he never intended to.

The music room connected to one of the parlours via a small courtyard that provided some light into the room. Because of the long corridors that ran around the outside of the hall, the natural light in each of the rooms on the ground floor came from small gardens that were laid out as four squares, like natural towers and were mostly overgrown through lack of care.

There were so few visitors that came to Duffleton Hall that most of the rooms were currently used and it was clear that the music room had not been used at all since Mr Brown had taken up residence. The furniture had large sheets covering all of it and a layer of thick dust was piled upon top of them and lay as a carpet over the wooden floor.

The quickest way to the back staircase was across the music room to the courtyard and then through the parlour that lay opposite it on the other side of the garden. There was a risk that he would be seen crossing the garden, but it would also be impossible for him to not leave behind footprints in the dust on the floor.

He thought for a moment and decided that it was worth the risk. If he stayed in the music room, it would not be long before it was searched either by the strangers or Mrs Hubbard, looking for Charles and Charlotte. He would surely be discovered then and he did not know that fate might await him then.

He quietly crept across the room, doing his best to disturb as little dust as he possibly could. When he reached the door to the courtyard it creaked loudly in his hand. He flinched and waited for someone to come and investigate the noise, but the shouting in the hallway drowned out all but the loudest of sounds.

He slipped into the garden and shut the door quickly behind him. Staying low, he crossed the garden and into the parlour opposite. The door didn't creak and it was almost the complete opposite to the music room.

It hadn't struck Mr Hunter as strange before, but standing in the room that looked so pristine and well-used was odd. The parlour was a room that would ordinarily be something given over to children to learn in or play in. It was a room that was almost inconsequential due to it's position and size, but it was clear it was being used by someone.

He heard footsteps in the corridor outside running back towards the front of the house and waited for them to fade before he went out into the hallway. It was as dim and quiet as it had been before.

He made his way to the rear staircase and slipped up them, hoping that he would find something up there that would explain what was happening at the Hall.

Lee and Stanley were far quicker at search rooms than Mr Hunter. The pair had developed a knack for knowing where important things were hidden or if something looked like it was going to be useful.

It was hard to say when or where they had acquired the skill but exploring the likes of Grangeback Manor and Buckingham Palace had given the pair experience that Mr Hunter would always lack.

The ground floor was easy to search for the most part, there were two rooms they had to avoid due to voices coming from within, but the rooms they could search were empty of anything interesting.

There was no one in the corridor to avoid so they managed to make it to the rear staircase with ease once they had finished searching the East Wing.

As they made their way up the stairs they heard a door open and close above them and for a moment the pair froze on the stair. If whoever was moving around on the floor above came down the staircase, there was nowhere for them to hide.

They would have to run and make it out of the house and disappear into the trees before whoever it was could catch them. Lee took a step back, ready to make good his escape, but the footsteps above began to move away from the rear stairs, and the pair breathed a sigh of relief.

Neither boy moved for a moment, making sure the footsteps had faded before they ascended to the floor above. They couldn't be certain which door the footsteps had come from, so they silently resolved to each take one side of the hallway each and search the rooms until they found something.

It was the second door that Stanley tried where he found one of the bedrooms had been repurposed into a strange study.

There was no desk in the room, but papers were stacked in piles on the floor, on the dressing table, and strewn across the bed. On the floor there was a piece of wood that seemed to have been drafted into service as a makeshift table top and there was a pen and ink pot sat upon it with a half-written letter.

Though Stanley had been educated and could read and write passably well, the words on the page looked completely alien to him. But there was something about the pages that made him grab some of the documents from the bed, where they would seemingly not be missed.

The rest of the rooms had very little to offer the two boys, there was nobody in them, although four of them were clearly being used.

There was no sign that Fortesque and Mr Brown were still in the hall. The only place left to search were the servants rooms in the basement below, but as they came back down the rear staircase, the voices at the front door were calming down and it was clear that they were running out of time.

Muriel was still nervously sitting in the kitchen and seemed surprised when the two boys re-entered the kitchen, one with arm fulls of paper.

"Oh please, you can't take those. They'll be so angry," Muriel whimpered.

"They'll never notice a few papers missing, don't worry," Stanley grinned as Mr Hunter joined them from the West Wing.

"I think our time is up. Muriel, please stay calm. We'll do all we can to help, but for now we need to leave," Mr Hunter said brightly and motioned for the Baker boys to follow him.

The three made straight for the treeline and used it to hide their presence as they snaked their way down towards the village and took the shortcut back to Grangeback Manor.

There had been no signs of Fortesque or Mr Brown on the upper or lower floors of Duffleton Hall, but Mr Hunter was not yet satisfied with his exploration of the house. There were still the rooms in the servants' quarters to search, and Mr Hunter was still curious as to where all the servants that worked at Duffleton Hall were.

He knew that there was a smaller staff that ran the house than Grangeback had, but he had only seen Muriel on his exploration and from what Lee and Stanley told him on the journey back home, they had not seen anyone either.

Lady Sarah was waiting anxiously for their return. Richard had dealt with the small number of patients that had required the attention of the doctor and made his way to Grangeback Manor.

Mrs Bosworth was fussing with tea and coffee, trying to take the whisky away from the brigadier and the doctor as she insisted that the pair needed clear heads to help Lady Sarah find Mr Brown.

Sylvia was walking Pattinson in the garden when the three came into view and Lee ran ahead to tell her what they had found and not found.

"The Egertons arrived around twenty minutes ago. Everyone is waiting in the library," she said curtly and led the way inside the house.

Mr Hunter knew that she was still upset with him over his refusal to take his fiancée's concerns seriously. He was certain that she still bore a grudge against him for leaving her after the loss of their child as well, but he could not dwell on Sylvia's low opinion of him when there was work to be done.

Dinner was delayed by an hour to allow Mr Hunter and the Baker boys time to tell everyone what they had found, or rather not found at Duffleton Hall. The papers were handed over to the doctor and the brigadier to inspect whilst the state of the Hall, the lack of servants and the four rooms in the East Wing being used.

What was more interesting to hear, was Thomas and Edward's account of their meeting with the new occupants of the Hall.

"Did you manage to force a physical confrontation?" Mr Hunter asked as he settled on the sofa beside Lady Sarah.

"No. They were far too guarded to be goaded. Even when Charlotte and Charles managed to slip past them and into the house," Edward said with a shake of his head.

"Yes, there sudden appearance almost saw me caught snooping," Mr Hunter chuckled and earned a look of reproach from Thomas.

"We were a diversion for you?" Thomas sounded insulted as he spoke.

"Though you were excellent at holding the attention of the strangers, it was not a necessary distraction. We could have searched the house during dinner, in fact that might have been preferable," Mr Hunter said, as though the idea had only just occurred to him.

"That's as maybe, but it seems in very poor taste to use us in such a fashion without our knowledge," Edward frowned.

"My apologies, gentlemen, I thought it for the best that the Baker boys and Mr Hunter exploring the Hall was kept secret. So as to not arouse the suspicion of the strangers," Lady Sarah said looking genuinely contrite.

"It seems like it would be ungallant for us to not accept your apology, especially as no harm was done," Thomas sighed.

"But surely the question is, did it bring any benefit?" Edward asked, clicking his tongue against his teeth.

"From the looks of these documents, it was extremely beneficial," the doctor said, almost absent-mindedly.

"You have found something interesting?" Sylvia asked as she tried to keep an eye on Baker boys and Egerton twins, who were all huddled in the corner of the library whispering to one another.

"These documents are written in a variety of different languages. There's French, Bavarian, Prussian, Italian, Greek, Spanish, Portuguese and Hungarian, and a few that seem to be in Arabic languages as well," the brigadier said thoughtfully.

"That is somewhat concerning," Thomas said slowly

as he moved over to take some of the documents to see for himself.

"The contents of the letters is strange, I suspect there are hidden messages in the text as they make little to no sense otherwise," the doctor sighed.

"There are hidden messages within the letters, but there are so vague that they mean very little to me," the brigadier said as he chewed his lip and narrowed his eyes.

"However?" Lady Sarah asked, knowing there was something the brigadier was not saying.

"However, there is a name that keeps appearing in the text," the brigadier said.

"A name?" Edward asked.

"Yes, one that seems to be significant, at least to be included in these messages. But it is also a name that is familiar to me; I can't quite place it though," the brigadier replied with frustration as he put the papers down and rubbed his forehead with his thumb and first two fingers.

"What is the name?" Mr Hunter asked.

"Armonis Cardel Puschat," the brigadier said.

Chapter 8

The documents were not a mystery that could be solved in one night. When Bosworth came in to call the household, and their guests, to dinner, the papers were all organised into piles - one for each language they were written in - and locked away in the brigadier's study.

Dinner was a rather muted affair as the brigadier was lost in thought, the Baker boys and Egerton twins were all too busy whispering to each other to speak to any of the adults and all Edward and Thomas wanted to speak of was the Hall and what could possibly have happened to Mr Brown.

Lady Sarah was also distracted as she tried to pull together threads of information that seemed to be completely divorced from one another.

Sylvia and Richard were still barely on speaking terms, and on the whole, it felt more like a dinner of strangers thrown together in awkward circumstances rather than close friends who had dined together many times before.

After dinner, the brigadier excused himself from the table and he and the doctor retired to his study for the rest of the night.

Thomas and Edward finally managed to pull Charlotte and Charles away from Stanley and Lee, and said their goodnights before returning to Tatton Park.

Lady Sarah and Sylvia took Pattinson to the library to play a few hands of cards so that Lady Sarah could think without interruption.

This left Mr Hunter and Richard with Lee and Stanley and nothing of use that any of the three could do, aside from retire to bed early. Richard made his excuses of an early start the following day and left the trap for his father to drive home in when he was finished with the brigadier.

At ten o'clock, Constable Evans called at the house to report what he had seen that day and his description of the strangers and their verbal altercation with the Egertons was almost identical to the story Thomas and Edward had told.

At eleven o'clock, Lady Sarah and Syliva made their way to bed, but the brigadier and doctor were too busy looking over the letters to worry about what time it was.

The messages within the letters were so vague that it was hard to discern any meaning. They were in different handwriting and the quality of paper used was different from letter to letter.

"If only we could access the room and read all the papers," the brigadier said after three fruitless hours of trying to make some sense out of the letters.

"That might be a little difficult to arrange at this point, though I am sure that Stanley and Lee would only be too happy to go back and retrieve more letters for you," the doctor said dryly.

"Your jests are in poor taste, Jack," the brigadier sighed and leant back in his chair.

"Better to jest than to allow your thoughts become so clouded by frustration that you cannot think straight," Doctor Hales shrugged and went to pour himself another drink.

He was sure the whisky was not helping them when it came to the trying to uncover whatever they were missing in the letters.

"My God, Jack! That's it! I must go to London at once.

Ring for Mrs Bosworth, I need her to pack and have Bosworth summoned to prepare the carriage," George Webb-Kneelingroach said as he leapt from his chair.

He was an aging man and far too well-fed to be much more than a lord of leisure in his twilight years, but every now and then, he had moments when he was capable of great action and energy that a man a third of his age would be envious of.

"What the devil?" the doctor cried out in surprise, almost spilling the decanter onto the highly polished floor.

"I know where I have heard that name before! I know where I know Armonis Cardel Puschat from," George said excitedly as he threw open the door to the study and stormed his way to his rooms.

The doctor put down the whisky and rang the bells, as the brigadier instructed, and waited for the rather sleepy pair of household domestics to appear.

"Doctor, what is happening?" Mrs Bosworth yawned.

"You master calls, he wishes a case packed for London and his carriage readied. He is to away tonight," the doctor replied with a wave of his hand in a direction of the staircase.

"At this time of night?" Mrs Bosworth exclaimed with weariness.

"It seems so. I shall trouble you no more this evening and see myself home," the doctor said and quickly made his way to the door and his waiting trap.

The groom that had drawn the short straw and been forced to stay up to care for the doctor's horse and have it ready for him to leave with, was now tasked with waving the other grooms and preparing the carriage for the brigadier.

He would not be spared from the early morning tasks of caring for the horses either, and would probably face some form of punishment from the head groom if he slept late or tried to skip any of his duties the following morning.

It would be a long night for him, as it would be for the driver that was now being roused from his bed by the firm and gentle hand of Bosworth.

Life at Grangeback Manor was many things, but it was never dull.

Chapter 9

Two days later, the rest of the Egerton family returned from London, and both Wibraham and William Egerton were just as concerned about Mr Brown's whereabouts as Lady Sarah was, especially when they were told of the strangers that had taken up residence at the Hall in his absence.

As politicians, the pair were both more acutely aware of the global climate and the tensions that existed between the different nation states, and which enemies of the Empire might be at work in such a quiet corner of the world.

With the brigadier's sudden, late night flight to London, Lady Sarah was now certain that whoever the strangers at Duffleton Hall were, they were part of a far larger plot with only malicious intent. However Mr Brown had ended up involved with them, he was in greater danger than even she had surmised and it was time to do something to bring him home safely.

The police constables had grown tired of days of

watching the Hall, in the wet, with nothing to report and pressure from the Chief Constable to end the vigil on the property and return his men to their normal duties could no longer be ignored.

Those that had come from Chester had returned to their homes and left Constable Evans and Constable Buckley to return to the police house in Stickleback Hollow.

Arwyn had solemnly promised that there was no reason for the police to be stationed outside of the manor house and they would much better watching the village for suspicious activity then focusing all their manpower watching the doors of Duffleton Hall.

Lady Sarah did not agree, but she could not argue logic against the feeling she had that something terrible would happen if the house was not being watched.

There had been no word from the brigadier since he had left for London, though this was not unusual. When he had been called away on the business of the Empire, he had been absent for months with no word on where he was or what had happened to him.

Richard had been to the manor to see if there was any news, but the doctor had remained at his surgery, and there was seemingly nothing else that could be done.

Lady Sarah was extremely restless and kept taking turns about the various gardens, even when it was raining, trying to quiet the uneasy feeling she had in her stomach. She hated waiting and the longer she had to wait to help her friend, the more frustrated she would become.

It wasn't until a further two days had passed that there was anything to report.

At 5 o'clock in the morning, there was a great hammering on the doors of Grangeback Manor. Pattinson was instantly roused and rather than growling, he happily barked a welcome at the people pounding on the door.

Bosworth was quick to answer the door, foregoing the usual politeness of dressing before he welcomed guests into the house.

Edward and Thomas were stood on the doorstep and both looked as though they had not slept in days. In the large carriage sat at the top of the driveway, all of the ladies of the Egerton family were waiting, worried faces peering out of the windows.

Mr Hunter was the first to come down, though Lady Sarah and Sylvia were not far behind. The Baker boys had managed to sleep through the noise of the pounding on the door and would not be woken unless Mrs Bosworth poured cold water over them.

"What on earth is happening?" Mr Hunter exclaimed as he saw Thomas and Edward.

"It's father and William," Thomas said with exasperation.

"What about them?" Sylvia frowned. She had refused to let Lady Sarah leave her bedroom without getting dressed first and was rather annoyed at having to fumble around in the dark to find clothing in a hurry.

"They've disappeared," Edward explained. The fear was plain on his face.

"Come inside, all of you, tell us all you can. Mrs Bosworth, rouse the Baker boys, send them to fetch the constables immediately," Lady Sarah said firmly and Mrs Bosworth went to raise the dead whilst Bosworth rushed outside in his nightshirt to help the footmen bring the ladies into the manor house.

The morning room was prepared and a fire had been lit in the grate by the maids who had to rise earlier than the rest of the household to prepare the fires and make sure that the occupants were warm.

Cooky was already in the kitchen, preparing the breakfast for the staff, but had delayed her normal routine to provide for the unexpected early morning guests.

As the ladies, the Egerton twins and Edward and Thomas were all shown into the morning room, there were two loud shrieks from the floor above and Lady Sarah could not help but smile.

"What was that?" Mary asked with alarm.

"Mrs Bosworth had to employ a rather cold method of waking up the two slug-a-beds," Mr Hunter explained.

When the fiancee of Edward looked confused by the reply, Sylvia simply said,

"A jug of cold water."

In spite of the seriousness of the situation, the guests from Tatton Park could not help but smile.

"Now come, tell us, what has happened," Lady Sarah said kindly as she motioned for Elizabeth and Lady Charlotte to join her on the larger sofa.

"Oh Sarah, we tried to persuade them to wait, but when we arrived home and Thomas and Edward told us that cousin Oliver was missing and that there were strangers barring entry to his home, they both were so angry and worried we couldn't stop them," Elizabeth explained. The normally unflappable matron of the Egerton family looked close to tears and grabbed hold of Lady Sarah's hand seeking reassurance.

"Peace, Elizabeth, peace," Lady Sarah soothed. "You know that once they have ideas in their heads, nothing can dissuade them."

"Yes, this is true. But why do they have to be so stubborn?" she cried.

"Where did they go?" Mr Hunter asked. It seemed an obvious question, and though he was certain he already knew the answer, it was better to ask than not.

"To Duffleton Hall, of course. They went to see these strangers who have taken over the house and demand some answers," Lady Charlotte said sharply, but almost instantly regretted her tone. "My apologies, Mr Hunter, but it really is most distressing."

"I do understand, Lady Charlotte," Mr Hunter said graciously.

"When did they go?" Sylvia asked. She ordinarily held her tongue when in the presence of other ladies, especially those who were of a higher social standing than she, but with the disappearance of so many of the Egerton family, the time to stand on ceremony seemed to have passed.

"Two days ago, just after we returned from town and Thomas and Edward told us of Oliver's disappearance," Elizabeth explained.

"They have been missing for two days? Why has it taken so long for you to worry about their whereabouts?" Mr Hunter asked with disbelief.

"When they did not return on the first day, we assumed that they had stayed for dinner or spent the night at Duffleton Hall. It was not beyond the realms of possibility that they had been able to gain entry to the Hall after speaking with t he strangers and discovered this was all just a misunderstanding," Lady Charlotte said, wringing her hands together as she spoke.

"But they clearly were not just guests at the Hall," Sylvia said dryly and earned a reproachful glance from Thomas.

"No, they were not. When they did not return home the following day for breakfast, we began to grow concerned. Then they were absent from the lunch table, so we went   directly to Chester to speak with the police," Lady Charlotte said earnestly.

"The Chief Constable," Elizabeth corrected her, and Sylvia rolled her eyes slighty.

"And what did the captain have to say?" Mr Hunter asked with a slight edge to his voice. The chief constable was a man named Captain Jonnes Smith, a man that had not always been easy to get on with. He did not approve of Lady Sarah's investigations, or her rather adventerous nature.

As far as the chief constable was concerned, ladies were not supposed to interfere in the work of men, and solving crimes and mysteries was not something women should be involved in.

"He was unwilling to come and investigate. He was already angry that time had been wasted by the constables watching the Hall where the only thing they observed was an argument between Thomas and Edward and the strangers who are staying there," Elizabeth explained.

"He suggested that William and Wilbraham had been called to town and that they would surely contact us soon with apologies and explain their absence, but we would have to wait on the whims of important men," Lady Charlotte said with irritation.

"The chief constable did send a message to Scotland Yard, asking them to call upon our house in town to see where my dear husband, and William are," Elizabeth said hopefully.

"But you were not convinced?" Lady Sarah asked gently.

"No. My husband does not disappear without word. No matter what has happened," Lady Charlotte said with certainty. Lady Sarah nodded, though she knew that it was not always possible for warning to be given to families when there were emergencies relating to the safety of the Empire.

The brigadier and the Baker boys mother, Angela, had both been called away on the business of the Empire for months without any word of where they were or when they would be back.

Even now, Lady Sarah did not know all that the brigadier had done whilst he was overseas, and she was almost certain that she did not want to know.

"And ever since we lost dear Wilbraham-" Elizabeth began, but her voice trailed off as she choked back more tears.

Wilbraham Egerton was not only her husband, but had been the name of her son as well. He had been a great friend to Lady Sarah, but he had been deployed overseas and died in service to the Crown.

His death had left a great hole in Lady Sarah's life, one she knew would never been filled by anyone else. He had been a great supporter, a confidente and had even been the one to convince Mr Hunter that he should embrace his feelings for Lady Sarah.

When he had died, Lady Sarah had already been feeling lost and alone, and to lose Wilbraham as well had felt like her whole world was collapsing around her. She did her best not to think about the loss of her friend, as when she did it was like her had died only hours ago. It was a wound in her heart that she knew would never heal and would carry with her for the rest of her life.

"Ever since our loss, we have all resolved to never disappear without first leaving word. We sent a telegram to our husbands and have had no reply," Lady Charlotte continued.

"And rather than go to the chief constable again, you

came here," Mr Hunter said understandingly.

"Yes, oh please, Sarah, you must help. I do not know what I will do without dear William and my darling husband," Elizabeth begged.

"Very well. I think it is time that Pattinson came with me to pay a visit to Duffleton Hall," Lady Sarah said firmly.

"Shall I come with you?" Mr Hunter asked with a slight edge of worry in his voice.

"No, I think it would be best if the doctor, Richard, Sylvia and Constable Evans came with me on this trip. If you will stay here with our guests for now, it would be for the best," Lady Sarah said slowly.

Mr Hunter nodded his agreement, though he wanted to protest. He did not like the idea of his fiancée walking head first into danger without him there to protect her.

He understood that the doctor, Richard and Sylvia had all been seen in her company by those in the house and that the presence of the constable would give them a measure of authority they had not had on their first visit.

"What I don't understand is why," Edward said with frustration.

"Why?" Sylvia asked with a slight frown.

"Why, when Thomas and I went with Charles and Charlotte, did they not take us prisoner or make us disappear? Why did it have to be father and brother?" Edward explained.

"Becasue the police were watching the front of the house," Mr Hunter sighed and shook his head. "It would not take much for them to be seen."

"Then where are they now? Why are they not watching the Hall still?" Lady Charlotte demanded.

"That is a question for the Chief Constable, I fear," Lady Sarah said with a sigh. She understood why Arwyn and Thompson had not wished to stay out in the wet watching nothing happen at the Hall. But she couldn't help but feel slightly vindicated for the second time in a few short days.

"Shall we leave at once?" Sylvia asked.

"No, we shall take breakfast with our guests first, and send a message to the doctor's residence to warn him and Richard of our need to visit the Hall," Lady Sarah replied calmly.

"Do you wish to send a warning to Constable Evans as well?" Mr Hunter asked lightly.

"No, I am sure the policemen will be awake and ready for duty," Lady Sarah said with a wisp of a smile upon her face.

Breakfast was a quiet affair, but Lady Sarah and Sylvia did not have long to enjoy it as the doctor and Richard arrived at the manor rather quickly to collect the ladies. Though Mr Hunter had agreed to not accompany them to Duffleton Hall, he did insist that Pattinson go with them.

The five set off for Duffleton Hall via the police house, leaving the Baker boys taking care of Charlotte and Charles and Mr Hunter to keep the Egerton family calm whilst they waited for news.

Constable Arwyn Evvans was not prepared for the party of visitors so early in the morning. He was even less prepared for the news that Wilbraham and William Egerton had both disappeared after going to Duffleton Hall.

He had never dressed so quickly in his life.

Lady Sarah sat silently in the doctor's trap, her back rigid, as they lurched along the road that led to the Hall.

Constable Evans had not dared to meet the eye of Lady Sarah since he was rudely awakened.

When they arrived at Duffleton Hall, Constable Evans and the doctor went to the door with Pattinson whilst Lady Sarah, Sylvia and Richard waited in the trap.

The now familiar face of one of the strangers appeared at the door and Patitnson let out a low growl that caused the doctor to place his hand on the collar of the dog, lest he decide to attack the stranger.

The constable cleared his throat and enquired about the whereabouts of Wilbraham and William, expecting the stranger to at least admit the two men had come to the Hall, but he was met with an instant denial of the two Egertons ever having reached the Hall.

The doctor tried a different tack, but was met with the same answer.

Lady Sarah watched the two men trying to force a confession from the stranger, but she could see that trying to question them on the doorstep of the Hall was a pointless endeavour.

Whoever these strangers were, they were dangerous and though there was no evidence that William and

WIlbraham had ever made it to Duffleton Hall, Lady Sarah knew, deep down, that the pair were in as much danger as Mr Brown and Fortesque.

Chapter 10

Lee and Stanley Baker were both tired of waiting in the manor for something to happen. Charlotte and Charles were both rather upset about the disappearance of their father and brother, which made the Baker boys even more determined to act.

Mrs Bosworth and Bosworth were too busy with their household duties to watch over the four children, and Cooky was trying to get her day back on track after the change in the order of the day with their unexpected guests.

Mr Hunter was doing his best to keep the other Egertons calm, so Lee, Stanley, Charles and Charlotte were the furthest thing from his mind or the minds of the other worried adults.

This made it easy for the four children to slip out of the house unseen. The Baker boys had spent the better part of the last three years getting to know every nook and cranny of Grangeback Manor, and could easily come and go as they pleased, but most of the time, they would be missed within minutes of their departure.

Lady Sarah was a watchful guardian and when she was absent, Sylvia, Cooky and Mrs Bosworth were as equally observant. The safety of the two boys was paramount, even with the dangerous mysteries they investigated.

They were close to turning 11 years old, and though they were somewhat educated, they both knew that it would not be long before their apprenticeships would involve a tutor and some formal education. In their exploration of the house, they had overheard Lady Sarah, Mr Hunter and the brigadier discussing their education, and Mr Hunter had been very firm about the pair not being sent away to boarding school.

The Baker boys had been most grateful for Mr Hunter wanting to keep them at the manor, and away from a school that he had been so miserable at. The pair often missed their adoptive mother, but she sent letters, and everyone at Grangeback had done their best to love and care for them, so much so, that in the time they had lived at the manor, they felt more at home than they had when living with their mother in her seamstress shop.

They both felt a little guilty about sneaking out of the house and disobeying Lady Sarah's orders to stay at the manor, but they also knew that they had a much better chance of exploring the house and evading the strangers whilst Lady Sarah was knocking on the front door than anyone else.

The trap would make better time on the road than the children did on foot, but they did not have to stick to the roads. The foursome ran across the Grangeback Estate, as fast as their legs could carry them.

They stumbled across the road and down through the village. Charlotte and Charles were not used to running so much, but the worry they felt for their father and brother kept them moving.

They left the village, all quite breathless and slowed to a walk as they made their way across the fields towards Duffleton Hall.

They had glimpsed the trap on their way through the village and knew they had time to walk the rest of the way and catch their breath.

Muriel was making breakfast in the kitchen when the four children opened the door and gave the poor cook a fright. She jumped out of her skin but managed to keep herself from screaming.

"What are you all doing here? Young master Charles, young Miss Charlotte, you shouldn't be here. It is not safe!" Muriel hissed and tried to shoo them out of the kitchen.

"We're here to find out what happened to our father and brother. We do not care how dangerous it is," Charles said defiantly.

"Please, it isn't safe," Muriel begged, but the four children ignored her and Charles led the way out of the kitchen towards the stairs that led down to the servant's quarters in the basement on the Hall.

Rather than split up to search, the four stayed together, but agreed that if they were discovered they would all scatter and run for help no matter what happened to the others.

Ordinarily, they would have expected to see all the servants of the Hall moving around, preparing for their day but the hallways were empty and the basement was oddly still.

They could hear voices coming from certain rooms and after listening at a number of doors, they discovered that most of the household staff were being forced to stay in their rooms or they would meet the same fate as Fortesque.

Lee was certain that if anyone was being held in the basement, they would be at the far end of the Hall, away from the rooms where the servants were all under house arrest.

Stanley was relieved that the servants all seemed to be accounted for, even if they were prisoners in their rooms, it was better than being missing.

They made their way down the corridor until they reached rooms with no voices coming from inside them. They checked each door in turn and found the majority of them were unlocked. Only three doors they came across were locked and those were the only rooms that Lee and Stanley were interested in searching.

As far as the Baker boys were concerned, there was no reason for the rooms to be locked, unless there was something inside the strangers were trying to hide.

It took fifteen minutes to pick the lock on the first of the doors and they found the room was empty. Clearly somebody had been in the room as a prisoner recently, but they were gone now. There was a makeshift bed on the floor, the smell of used chamberpots that had been left unemptied, and trays of food that had been left in the corner of the room to rot.

The second lock took less time to pick, but the room was in a similar state to the first. It was clearly where someone had been held prisoner, but it was now empty too.

The third lock took the longest, but as the door swung open, the four were glad they had persisted with the lockpicking as in the room was Fortesque the butler.

"Children?" he frowned as he looked up, clearly expecting his captors rather than an unlikely rescue party.

"Fortesque! What have they done to you?" Charlotte gasped. There were cuts on his face and neck that were covered with dried blood, and he was clearly in a great deal of pain. His skin was washed out and he was in need of a bath.

"Miss Charlotte?" he asked with confusion as she came to his side and began to untie his feet and hands.

"Yes, and Charles too, and the Baker boys from Grangeback Manor. We came to rescue you," she said.

"No, you must go. It is too dangerous here. They already took your father and brother. They can't take you too," Fortesque said as he tried to pull away from his rescuers.

"Then you saw the Egertons?" Lee asked brightly. "Does that mean you know what happened to them? And what about Mr Brown?"

"I don't know what happened to the master. They keep alluding to holding him somewhere, but I don't know where. But Master William and Master Wilbraham, they were taken last night. It was about midnight and these man came. They were armed with all manner of weapons you can imagine, and wearing strange uniforms. They took them both. I watched through the keyhole. I was certain they were coming back for me too," Fortesque said and shook his head.

"Come on, we'll help you walk. Lady Sarah is outside with the doctor. They will help you," Stnaley said firmly as he took one of the butler's arms around his shoulders and Lee took the other arm.

The pair lifted the butler to his feet and helped him walk towards the door. Charles and Charlotte went ahead of the three of them, keeping an eye out for the strangers and Mrs Hubbard.

They had almost reached the stairs when a cough

came from behind them.

"What is this then?" a heavily accented voice asked with amusement. Lee and Stanley froze, but Fortesque had been prepared for this moment.

He pushed the two boys away from him and hurled himself backwards towards the owner of the voice.

"Run!" he yelled at the children, who did not need to be told twice.

They scrambled up the stairs whilst the stranger struggled under the deadweight of the butler. A cry for help in a foreign language rang out and they knew it wouldn't be long before the other strangers found them.

They bolted for the kitchen and out the door without a word to Muriel. The cook simply stared at the children as they ran past.

"Where do we go?" Charlotte asked.

"Make for the road. Lady Sarah can't be far away," Lee said and led the four of them over the fields of the Grangeback Estate and towards the road to the village.

The sound of hooves plodding along the road could be heard before they saw the trap. Pattinson barked and caused the trap to be brought to a stop as the four children barrelled into the road and all tried talking at once.

The horse was startled by the sudden appearance of the frantic children, but Richard managed to keep it from bolting.

"What on earth are you all doing out here?" the doctor asked with alarm.

"You had to explore the Hall again?" Sylvia asked dryly, looking at the two sets of twins with an unimpressed look on her face.

"Yes, we're sorry, but we found Fortesque!" Lee said.

"He's at the Hall still?" Lady Sarah asked with concern.

"Yes, we rescued him but he sacrificed his own freedom so we could escape when we were discovered," Stanley said.

"But more importantly, he saw father and brother. He said armed men in uniforms came to take them from the Hall in the night," Charles said, struggling to catch his breath.

"What do we do?" Arwyn asked as he looked back at the Hall. "I can arrest them based on everything that the children found."

"No, that is too dangerous for you to do alone. We don't need you disappearing too," the doctor said gruffly.

"The doctor is right. But I do not like the idea of Fortesque being a prisoner in the Hall," Lady Sarah sighed as she alighted from the trap and motioned for Sylvia and Pattinson to join her.

The dog leapt out and seemed glad of the chance to stretch his legs.

"Take the children back to Grangeback and make sure everyone is safe there. We will go down to the village and warn everyone to stay inside and lock their doors," Lady Sarah instructed.

"I will come with you," Arwyn said and jumped out of the trap. "We'll cover more ground with three of us."

"Very well. Be quick, Richard and the pair of you should stay at the manor for now as well. If anyone needs you, doctor, I will have them come to the manor," Lady Sarah said firmly, and neither Richard, nor the doctor argued.

Chapter 11

The trap disappeared down the road quickly, leaving Lady Sarah, Sylvia, Arwyn and Pattinson to continue on foot.

With the children's flight from the Hall and nearly being caught, Lady Sarah was convinced that there would be pursuers searching the grounds of the estate and that it would be best if they hurried on their way.

Though she carried her revolver in her bag and had both Pattinson and Arwyn with her, she did not want to engage in a confrontation with these strangers where they had the advantage.

"Come, we must be quick," Lady Sarah urged and the three adults and the dog set off at a brisk pace down the road. After they had walked a short distance, they cut across the fields and made good time to the village.

There were no signs of anyone from the Hall following them, but Lady Sarah did not want to risk being out in the open longer than they had to be.

As soon as they reached the edge of the village, the three split up and went to visit every house and business in Stickleback Hollow. There were no strangers in any of the houses and all the residents knew to take any warnings given by Lady Sarah - whether directly or indirectly - were to be taken seriously.

Her ladyship had not wished to spread panic amongst the village residents, but she knew that underplaying how dangerous these strangers were would only lead to more people being unnecessarily placed in harm's way.

"We tell them that they need to stay indoors, that four people are missing and we do not want their names to number amongst the missing. Once we have apprehended those with malicious intent, everyone is free to go about their business," Lady Sarah had said, with a rather firm tone, and both Sylvia and Arwyn had agreed that it would be for the best.

There was no arguments from any of the people they spoke to. Those who were alone in their homes and felt they wanted to be with others were escorted to friends' houses, or joined the trio on their rounds about the village and would come back to the manor for protection.

The last person in Stickleback Hollow who knew that anything was amiss was Constable Thompson Buckley and he was only too happy to lock up the police house and join the small throng of people walking to the manor.

"What do we do now?" Sylvia whispered to her mistress as they walked at the head of the small group of people. She did not want to be overheard as she knew that even the tiniest amount of doubt in what they were doing would cause a panic.

"We lay a trap for our visitors," Lady Sarah said with a slight smile curling at the corner of her mouth.

"You think the strangers will come to Grangeback?" Sylvia asked with alarm, but managed to keep her voice low.

"I think that our strangers have friends and that is the reason they knew where the police were, when the house was being watched and when it was not. For Mr Brown, and the two Egertons to all be removed from the house without being seen, there has to be more than the handful of people we know are at the Hall involved. It would be impossible for them to make our friends vanish in such a fashion without others to help them," Lady Sarah explained quietly.

"And having seen the children trying to save Fortesque, they will discover that they are at Grangeback and know they have told us what Fortesque said and now have to move to silence us all," Sylvia concluded.

"Precisely. So we must prepare and part of that preparation is ensuring the safety of all the people of the village first. No matter how many they send against the house, they will come against us on the ground floor first. We shall hold them there and spring our trap. The servants and the villagers we shall ensure are all upstairs and safe from any harm," Lady Sara said firmly.

"And what trap would you spring on invaders?" Sylvia asked.

"They do not know what our numbers are, nor our armourments. They will come expecting us to be unprepared for them and to fall without resistance. We shall show them how mistaken they are," Lady Sarah shrugged.

They continued the walk to Grangeback in silence, and the doors to the manor were thrown open for the group as they approached.

The doctor and Richard had allowed the Baker boys and Egerton twins to explain what they had discovered at

Duffleton Hall and it had taken all Mr Hunter's powers of persuasion to keep Thomas and Edward from marching on the Hall for vengeance.

"What do you intend to do?" Thomas asked abruptly the moment Lady Sarah stepped through the door.

"Gather everyone in the ballroom and explain what is about to happen. Sylvia, I will need you to go to Chester at once," Lady Sarah said, completely unfazed by the tone Thomas was using.

He was normally quite calm and easy to talk with. Both Thomas and Edward had always had a good rapport with her ladyship, and to hear either of the gentlemen being short with Lady Sarah was unusual to say the least.

Thomas looked at her ladyship with a slight confused look on his face but nodded and with the help of Mr Hunter, Richard and Edward, gathered the household and the guests all into the ballroom to await Lady Sarah.

"Doctor, go with her. I need you to go to the police house and in the loudest way, express concerns about the safety of the children as they have not only seen the strangers in Duffleton Hall but they also found one of the missing men. Make it clear that the police are to attend the manor tomorrow morning and take action to rescue Fortesque from his captors," Lady Sarah said in a low voice to ensure no one else overheard her.

"Very well. Shall we return here once we have delivered the message?" the doctor asked.

"Yes, but when you do, go to the stables and use the side door," Lady Sarah said.

"Very well, we shall go at once," Sylvia nodded and the pair left without another word.

Lady Sarah sighed and shook her head as she watched them go. She did not want to believe that any amongst the Cheshire police could be in league with these strangers, but it was the only conclusion that made sense to her. Amongst the good officers of the law, there were some bad ones and though that could not be helped, she would use it to her advantage.

"Are you alright?" Mr Hunter asked with concern as he looked at his fiancée as she stood in the middle of the entrance hall.

"I shall be, but we must all get through tonight," she replied, and taking Mr Hunter's arm, made her way to the ballroom.

Chapter
12

Brigadier George Webb-Kneelingroach was not a man to waste time. At least he did not waste time when the safety of the realm was in jeopardy.

He had recognised the name Armonis Cardel Puschat and the moment he had placed the name, he had made for the Foreign Office. The men that worked in those halls of power had more duties than to simply manage trader with foreign nations and diplomatic solutions to problems that might occur from time-to-time.

They were also spies and information gatherers, messengers and a far deadlier force in the British Empire than the military.

It was the Foreign Office who had directed George, Mr Henry Cartwright, Captain Jonnes Smith and Miss Angela Baker to all depart for India, and it was at the Foreign Office that George would find the answers he needed as to who the strangers at Duffleton Hall were.

The name Armonis Cardel Puschat was one that the

brigadier had come across many years ago. It was the alias for one of the agents of the British Empire. He had been serving in India and had been a contact for the brigadier when he had transferred from his frontline military duties to a more covert role.

It had been a name that he had filed away in the back of his mind and hoped he would never come across again. He had been a young man at the time and one that was always rushing head long into danger. He was a valuable asset to the Crown and to see his name listed amongst the papers spelt trouble.

When he entered the halls of the Foreign Office, a polite young man tried to turn him away as the brigadier did not have an appointment and the Foreign Office was not a place that people could simply walk into, off the street, and expect to see someone.

But the brigadier was used to dealing with young men like the clerk. They were from rich families, well-educated, but disposable as far as the line of succession and inheritance was concerned.

"Young man, go to the third office on the second floor of this building, knock twice and Sir Reginald Cook will ask you to enter. When he does, say the name Armonis Cardel Puschat to him. I shall be waiting down here for you to come and collect me," the brigadier said with a firm and commanding tone.

The clerk looked at the brigadier with suspicion, but did as the brigadier had instructed. He walked at a leisurely pace and if it had not been for the sound of Sir Reginald Cook's voice echoing down the corridors of the building, the brigadier would have thought that the young man had gone to wait somewhere else until the brigadier grew bored and left.

The clerk soon scurried down the stairs, his skin as white as bleached paper, and with a distinct stammer, bade the brigadier to follow him.

"George!" Sir Reginald said with relief when he laid eyes on the brigadier. "You snivelling little fool, when this man comes to call, you show him to my office immediately!" Sir Reginald roared at the clerk, who mumbled apologies before backing out of the room as fast as he could without falling over.

"Trouble with the new boy?" George asked with slight amusement.

"Honestly, George, these boys fresh out of Oxford and Cambridge, they have no knowledge of the real world. No understanding of the powers at work. Sometimes I wonder if we wouldn't be better recruiting some of the soldiers that fought Napoleon and have been left begging in the streets," Sir Reginald sighed and shook his head with disgust.

"I have long said that those men would serve us well. They may not speak without an accent but they can be very convincing double agents, if they pay is right," George shrugged.

"Perhaps. But how far does loyalty to Queen and Country carry those men?" Sir Reginald sighed.

"It carried them across the fields of Flanders, Portugal and Spain under the command of King George. It took them to the horrors of Waterloo and Trafalgar and brought them home again," the brigadier replied. "It took them to the depths of the darkest parts of India and home."

"I see your point. Perhaps it is something we should consider. But what is all this about Armonis Cardel Puschat? Why use that name to get my attention? Were you just teaching the little snot a lesson?" Sir Reginald asked as he moved to the drinks cabinet and pour two large brandys for them to talk over.

"No. There's a situation in my village. A young friend of my ward, the American cousin of the Egertons, he disappeared," George explained as he let the aroma of the brandy fill his nostrils.

"Ah, and you thought Lady Sarah was perhaps the reason for the disappearance? A young man slighted in love?" Sir Reginald asked with a slight grin. "Come George, you think I wouldn't know something as simple as that? The love triangle between your son, the American and your ward has been quite the subject of gossip amongst the ladies here about."

"As gratifying as it is to know that, I foolishly did believe so," George replied with a slight edge to his voice. "But when her ladyship went to call at Duffleton Hall to enquire after Mr Brown, he was not only not at home, there were four strangers, by a reliable count, there instead."

"And how does Armonis Cardel Puschat fit into this? Was he amongst their number?" Sir Reginald frowned.

"No. His name was on some papers that the Baker boys retrieved from the Hall when they went to search it with my son," the brigadier replied.

"By God, you do have quite the little band of firebrands on your hands, don't you? If I could have them all on my pay, imagine what they could do for the Empire!" Sir Reginald said with glowing admiration.

"I would rather my family would be kept out of these matters as much as possible. Her ladyship already uncovers danger wherever she goes. I do not need to force her into it's path," George said dryly.

"Quite so, quite so. Then you suspect Armonis Cardel Puschat is in danger or at least compromised. That is most disturbing news indeed," Sir Reginald took a long sip from his brandy and held the dark liquid on his tongue whilst he thought.

"Is he deployed in France by any chance?" the brigadier asked coyly and watched Sir Reginald almost spit his drink across the room.

"How the devil did you know that?" the civil servant asked with surprise. "Wait, I forget who I am talking to. Don't tell me how you know. It will only depress me."

"On the contrary. It was either France or Prussia. The strangers at the Hall seemed to go out of their way to drop

German amongst their English, which even struck our village doctor as rather odd. It also made little sense for Prussian spies to be in a country where our own queen and her prince are so tied to the Deutscher Bund through the house of Hanover," the brigadier grinned.

"I see, then our spies are rather foolish, or hoped to find themselves amongst ignorant rabble who would sew discord, and even stir up opposition to the heritage of our monarch," Sir Reginald mused.

"Not so foolish then. Especially given the anti-royalist sentiments that have circled around the northern cities, especially Manchester," the brigadier said seriously.

"So Frankish spies have landed upon our shores and are bent on undermining us," Sir Reginald shook his head.

"Is it simply trying to undermine the monarchy, or is there something else at work?" the brigadier frowned.

"Our military growth is upsetting the French. With the crippling of their navy by Nelson and our admirals and the destruction of Napoleon at the hands of the Duke of Wellington, the French have been somewhat upset with us. As they can't attack us and prevail with military might, they are set on undermining our economy, foreign trade, relationships, all with an aim at stopping our military expansion and weakening us," Sir Reginald explained.

"Which is why Armonis Cardel Puschat was dispatched to France, to see what he could learn of their plans and we could then counter them," the brigadier sighed.

"Indeed, but as it stands, we shall have to remove him immediately. Perhaps it is a time to find some veterans who could serve as spies, disgruntled men looking to hurt Britain for turning her back on them and earning the trust of the French only to report back to us. The idea has potential," Sir Reginald said thoughtfully.

"French spies must have a network, if we have found four of them at Duffleton Hall, we should work quickly and do our best to find them all before they can run to ground," the brigader replied.

"Yes, quite so. I will make arrangements to send a regiment back with you, and some of our agents to work quickly to find out all they can. Be swift, my friend, we cannot afford for any of them to escape," Sir Reginald said earnestly.

Chapter
13

The discussion in the ballroom did not go quite as Lady Sarah had imagined it would. With the revelation that the manor would be under attack by those who were at least working with those who were responsible for the disappearance of Fortesque, Mr Brown and the elder Egertons, none of the able bodied men in the household agreed to locking themselves in the rooms on the upper floors to wait until the danger had passed.

Bosworth was by far the most offended by such a suggestion. The ladies agreed to all hide on the upper floors with the older men from the village to protect them should anyone slip past those defending the ground floor.

Charlotte and Charles refused to hide if Stanley and Lee were facing the danger of an assault on the manor, much to their mother's chagrin. Thomas and Edward tried to persuade them to hide with the others, but it was to no avail. The pair had found Fortesque, been into the den of the enemy twice, and would not back down now in the face of any that would try to harm those they held dear.

Weapons were in short supply, given the number of men that had chosen to defend the manor. The guns, that were used for hunting, were taken from the cabinets in the brigadier's study and distributed to those with the experience to wield them.

A chair was brought in to the middle of the entrance hall for Lady Sarah to sit upon with Pattinson by her side. The men with guns fanned out along the stairs and aimed their guns at the front door.

Mr Hunter and the two constables went to the back of the house to guard the kitchen entrance to the house, whilst the Egertons and Richard went to the side door from the stables to prevent anyone coming through it.

The french windows in the lounge, drawing room and ballroom were all defended by men from the village, so armed with clubs, others with the antique swords that decorated the walls and suits of armour the brigadier had collected over the years.

The sound of the trap coming up the driveway and pulling round to the stable heralded the arrival of Sylvia and the doctor, who came to stand with Lady Sarah in the entrance hall.

The Baker boys, Charlotte and Charles seemed to have completely disappeared, but Lady Sarah knew that they would be hiding in the walls somewhere, watching everything, ready to leap out at the opportune moment.

"Did all go well?" Lady Sarah asked as Sylvia came to stand at her side.

"It did. The doctor demanded to speak with the Chief Constable and did so in the middle of the police headquarters, in front of many policemen, members of the public and criminals," Sylvia said with a satisfied smile on her face.

"Good. Then we shall soon have company," Lady Sarah said, as her hand briefly paused whilst stroke Pattinson's head.

The Japanese hunting dog was sat right in front of her and not only was ready to protect his mistress, but was helping to keep her anxiety in check.

This was not the first time that men had come to attack Grangeback Manor, and they were certainly far more prepared for this assault than the previous one, but it did not mean that all those waiting inside the house were not nervous.

The halls of Grangeback lapsed into a tense silence. There were no lights in any of the windows and the stillness was so intense that it made everyone afraid to move even the smallest amount.

It felt like hours had passed since Sylvia and Doctor Hales had arrived back at the manor, but it was only half an hour in reality, when there was the sound of pick scrapping in the lock of the front door.

Lady Sarah's back stiffened and Pattinson let out a low growl.

When the door swung open shade cloths were pulled off lamps held by the kitchen boys, positioned between the men with guns on the stairs and from the light cast, five figures standing in the doorway were surprised to see Lady Sarah and the men of Stickleback Hollow waiting for them.

"Good evening," Lady Sarah said with all the civility she could muster. Her fingers were digging deeply into the fur around Pattinson's neck to make sure the dog did not lunge at the men in the doorway.

"Mein Gott," one of the men said with surprise, but rather than trying to run away, he stepped into the house.

"Did you expect this to be a surprise?"

"No, but those men you have approaching the house from other directions may well be in for a surprise," Sylvia replied curtly.

"Women are really such simple creatures. They do not have the capacity to think well enough to execute any complex strategy, it is very sad to think that you assume we have been cornered by this show of force," another of the figures said, addressing the doctor instead of Lady Sarah.

"We have not come to kill anyone, but we shall ensure that you are silenced," the first figure said, directing his comments to Lady Sarah.

"I do not think you will succeed in such a foolish course of action," the doctor said, shaking his head.

"Then you, sir, are just as simple as these women," the second man said and he lunged forward.

Lady Sarah released her hand from the dog's neck and Pattinson leapt forwards. It took a moment for him to leap at the man advancing on his mistress and sink his teeth into his enemy's arm.

So big was the Akita, that he dragged the stranger to the ground in a single motion and refused to let go.

The sound of glass shattering around the entrance hall and from the other rooms around the manor caused the men armed with guns to rush from their high ground to defend the ground floor of the manor.

Chaos erupted in every room as the number of those assaulting the manor threatened to overwhelm its defenders. Lady Sarah did not move from her chair as the men fought around her. Sylvia stood at her side and only had to swing a few well-placed punches and one effect knee to remain in her place.

Two men managed to get past the men in the hallway and began to run up the stairs, put as they reached the landing, a panel on the wall swung open and the Baker boys and Egerton twins leapt out and pushed the two men backwards, causing them to fall backwards down the staircase.

"We shall not be beaten so easily," Thomas' voice yelled from somewhere deep in the household and it was clear that every man that fought to defend Grangeback felt the same way.

Lady Sarah watched, calmly and serenely, as the fighting cointuned around her.

"Go," she whispered to Sylvia. Her companion looked at her with a quizzical expression, but did not question her instruction. Sylvia dodged through the fighting and made her way up the stairs to where the Baker boys and Egerton twins were.

"You have left yourself vulnerable," the first stranger said from behind Lady Sarah. "Throw down your weapons and I will not harm the lady."

Lady Sarah smiled to herself and sighed.

"It would be pointless to try and silence those of us in this household. The brigadier left for London days ago. Whatever happens to those of us here, your identity has no doubt already been uncovered and there shall be no corner of the Empire where you shall be safe," her ladyship said with a slight shake of her head.

"If that is so, then why all this? Why the invasion of the household? Why bring us here?" the first man asked, his voice stuttering slightly.

"You took those who are dear to us, and we will not rest until they are returned," Edward said from behind the man and delivered a swift blow to the back of his head.

The men of Stickleback Hollow had defended the

house well and those that had attempted to infiltrate through the windows and doors on the rest of the ground floor had all been dispatched and were now being dragged, unconscious into the entrance hall.

The kitchen boys had set down their lamps and fetched ropes so the grooms could tie up the men. There were a number of injuries that the doctor had to attend to, and the men that had been pushed down the stairs needed immediate attention.

But the defenders had escaped with only minor injuries, much to the relief of the women who were waiting upstairs.

Sylvia went to open the doors and allow the women to come and see the victorious men as Mr Hunter and Richard did their best to keep Edward and Thomas from questioning the men about the whereabouts of their family members.

Arwyn and Thompson made to leave the manor for Duffleton Hall to retrieve any who still remained there and rescue Fortesque but as they stepped out into the night, they saw torches in the night, approaching the manor.

"What is that?" Constable Buckley asked nervously.

"I do not know," Constable Evans replied with alarm. "Your ladyship, perhaps the men with guns could come outside a moment?"

Lady Sarah frowned and made her way outside to see what was wrong.

"Reinforcements?" Thompson asked.

"No, they can't be. Why would they wait to come in waves?" Lady Sarah said with a frown.

"I suspect that my father may have something to do with that. Listen," Mr Hunter said as he came to join them.

They all strained their ears to listen and were rewarded with the sound of rhythmic marching growing louder as the lights approached.

It took only a handful of minutes to pass before the carriage of the brigadier came into view and behind him was a regiment of soldiers.

"Good evening," the brigadier greeted his ward, son and two policemen with surprise, and then his eyes fell on the house. "What on earth has happened?"

Chapter
14

The brigadier was less than impressed with the state of his house, but he was glad that they were safe and some of the French spies had been exposed.

The soldiers of the regiment took the spies from the house and the brigadier explained who the men were as they were taken away and those who were not injured began cleaning up of the debris and damage to the manor.

Arwyn, the brigadier and Constable Buckley were spared from cleaning duty as they had business at Duffleton Hall to attend to.

Mrs Hubbard and the two strangers who had remained behind were arrested, and though the four men who had taken over Duffleton Hall were not willing to talk, Mrs Hubbard was only too willing to tell everything she knew in order to save her own skin.

There were two spies amongst the police force in Chester that she named, who were arrested almost immediately, and explained how the strangers in the Hall had known when it was being watched.

Richard and Doctor Hales took Fortesque into their home to help the butler recover from his ordeal, and the rest of the staff at Duffleton Hall were greatly relieved to finally be free.

Wilson's Inn was busy that evening with the men who had taken part in the defence of Stickleback Hollow telling tales of their bravery and the Duffleton Hall servants telling stories of their imprisonment.

The brigadier was busy for several days following the arrest of the spies and he set to work rooting out all those that were connected to the spy ring and ensuring that the French plans had been well and truly thwarted.

A week after they had been taken, Wilbraham and William were returned home to Tatton Park, and Mr brown returned home to Duffleton Hall.

Mrs Hubbard had been quick to give up the location they had been taken to and the three men had been given the best of medical care. Wilbraham Egerton had refused to return home until he had help the brigadier to end the French spy presence in the north, and William had known that he could not go home without his father.

Mr Brown was in considerably poorer condition than his cousins as he had been a prisoner far longer and the tortue he had endured for information that could be useful to the French had been relentless.

Lady Sarah had refrained from visiting with him at the hospital and did not call upon him when he returned home. She was simply glad that he was alive and returned without too much lasting damage.

Three days after his return home, Mr Brown came to call at Grangeback Manor. He was surprised to see most of the windows on the ground floor were boarded up and was treated to the tale of the battle of Grangeback from Lee and Stanley Baker.

Lady Sarah was out riding when he called, but he was happy to wait for her return. Mr Hunter came to speak awkwardly with him, and was very much relieved when he could excuse himself from the conversation.

"Mr Brown, this is a surprise," Lady Sarah said as she came in, cheeks flushed and hair somewhat matted by the wind.

"I am sorry to call unanounced, but perhaps we could dispense with the Mr? We have been friends for a long time now, and I like to think, almost engaged," Mr Brown drawled warmly.

"Very well, then, Oliver," Lady Sarah smiled and invited her guest to sit with her.

"Good. I came to say thank you to you, and to apologise as well," Mr Brown said as he sat on the sofa beside her.

"You have no need to do either. I fear though, I owe you an apology," Lady Sarah said with a shake of her head.

"You have never owed me anything," Mr Brown said and shook his head. "But you are wrong in that I don't need to do either. I need to thank you because if you hadn't been so certain something was wrong, then I may well have died at the hands of those French spies. You didn't give up on trying to find me when everyone told you that you should. I am grateful to have a friend that is so tenacious. And I should apologise because it was my own stupidity that allowed those men to take my household so easily."

"How did they come to be at the Hall? That is something that no one has been able to discover," Lady Sarah asked with genuine curiosity.

"It was Mrs Hubbard. I needed a new housekeeper

and the perfect one appeared, and she wanted very little in the way of compensation, but she did need a bed for her brother whilst he was searching for employment. He seemed a decent man when I met him, he asked if some friends come join us for dinner one evening and when we were sitting drinking brandy and I was doing my best to drown my sorrows, they struck and I found myself being locked in my own bedroom, gagged and trussed up like a turkey," Mr Brown explained. "I'd rather spare you the details of what happened after that."

"Well I am grateful to be spared, but the brigadier will want to know what you told me. Mrs Hubbard has been a little too helpful with her information, but it seems she has left out a great deal," Lady Sarah replied and went to ring the bell.

"Before I do, there is one other thing I wanted to say to you, Sarah," Mr Brown said as he stood up and walked over to where she stood.

He gently took her hand in his and looked at her with a great deal of regret in his eyes.

"Please, do not be sad," Lady Sarah said as she squeezed the hand holding hers. "I am sorry for all the hurt I have caused you and I hope that our friendship will be able to endure regardless."

"I'm not sad. Well, I am a little sad, but it's not what you might think. I am hurt because I became a burden to you in all this. I barely knew you when I proposed to you, and you were in a great deal of pain over Mr Hunter. I was swept away by the idea of you and not by who you are. I was looking for what I wanted to see and when I saw some of it in you, I couldn't help myself. Thomas and Edward were both quite insistent upon it as well, but I rushed into a proposal without any thought to how you were feeling. I do not know if that has meant that we have both missed out on what could have been something beautiful and glorious betweeen us, but I do know that a lot of my pain is of my own making," Mr Brown explained.

"You saw me for who I was and you accepted me without any reservation and you were wise enough to hold back from me. I am grateful to you for that. But I would like us to start over as friends. If you think that is possible."

"I do not think we need to start over, Oliver. But perhaps you and Alexander might?" Lady Sarah said.

"Perhaps, though I think with time, we shall be far

better friends and our days of rivalry will be long past. If you do not think we need to start over as friends, then I have a promise to make to you. No matter what the situation, when you need me at your side, I will always be there," Mr Brown said seriously.

"That does not sound like the promise a friend makes," Lady Sarah frowned.

"It is the promise that only true friends can make and keep," Mr Brown grinned. Though Lady Sarah was not certain she believed him. She accepted the promise and was glad that her friend was home once more and there were no more strangers in Stickleback Hollow.

The mysteries aren't over in Stickleback Hollow! Lady Sarah returns for more super sleuthing in the next volume of the Mysteries of Stickleback Hollow…

Her wedding day is finally here, but she might not make it down the aisle. An assassin is lurking to turn the happiest day of her life into her last.

Get _Wedding in Stickleback Hollow_ now!

Want to stay up to date with all the latest news from Stickleback Hollow, then you can sign up to my newsletter here.

Love the Mysteries of Stickleback Hollow? Not caught up

with the rest of the series, then jump back to *A Thief in Stickleback Hollow*, Book 1 in the Mysteries of Stickleback Hollow and see how it all began.

Want to help a reader out? Reviews are crucial when it comes to helping readers choose their next book and you can help them by leaving just a few sentences about this book as a review. It doesn't have to be anything fancy, just what you liked about the book and who you think might like to read it.

Scan the QR Code below or visit Strangers in Stickleback Hollow.

If you don't have time to leave a review or don't feel confident writing one, recommending a book to your family, friends and co-workers can help them choose their next book, so feel free to spread the word.

Historical Note

This historical note is a surprisingly difficult one to write because most of the historical elements I have included have been covered before. The Egertons of Tatton Park, their positions in politics, their family relations etc. So my apologies that it is rather brief and not quite as detailed as previous historical notes.

The French really were trying to stop the military growth of the British following the end of the Napoleonic Wars but there is no evidence they ever used a spy network to accomplish this. Common sense might dictate that spies ere used to do this, but there is no empirical evidence to suggest that any of the events that take place in this book are based in reality.

Wilbraham and William Egerton were both politicians and important men in Cheshire as well as the UK government, but neither of them were kidnapped and imprisoned by

French spies posing as Prussians.

Armonis Cardel Puschat is a complete fiction, alongside Sir Reginald Cook. Neither men existed, but it was fun to bring so more depth to the brigadier and his time spent working on the information gathering side of the military and not the front lines.

A great deal of men were left injured as a result of the naval battles and military battles that took place during the late 1700s and early 1800s. The Regency period is especially romanced by fiction, but the reality is that a lot of men were left with missing limbs, and no work to come home to. A lot become homeless or simply died from their injuries. A good number did develop anti-government and anti-royalist sentiments. The idea to turn them into agents to work on behalf of the government and use their hatred to convince the enemies of the Empire they could be trusted to spy for them is something that is used throughout fiction, and may well have happened, but again, there is no evidence that this was ever common practice.

The assault on Grangeback was somewhat overexaggerated with the number of spies that were gathered to silence those at the manor. It was a little over-the-top, I admit, but it was important to illustrate just how large these spy networks can become, and how they can be part of any organisation. In fact, it is almost essential for them to be part of powerful and integral institutions, such as the police force, to help them carry out their missions.

But with Mr Brown freed from his captivity, the way is now clear for Lady Sarah and Mr Hunter to finally wed.

A Note About Gen AI

Dearest readers, if there is one thing I absolutely hate with every fibre of my being, it is Generative AI. It is a scourge, a cancer, not just for its complete disregard for the creative arts, human rights, and copyright, but for the unbelievable damage it is doing to the planet, society, and the brains of all those who have been conned into thinking it is the way to the future or even necessary in their lives.

I have never and will never use Generative AI in any form. Please remember the words of many authors, like myself, have been stolen and are now being spat back out. Our unique voices have been stolen, and when we are accused of using these terrible machines because what we have written "sounds like AI", it is because it has stolen our voices, our words, our styles. We do not sound like Generative AI.

Gen AI is mimicking us in the poorest fashion. So when you read my words, know you are supporting a human, one who pays other humans for their time, talent, and commitment, to bring her books to you; who spends sleepless nights agonising over word choice and plot direction, who bores her best friend with endless questions and complaints about this stupidly hard and wonderful profession, and who will never give up the challenge and joy of writing these books herself.

Please respect how much I loathe and detest Generative AI and do not feed my work into Gen AI platforms such as Anthropic and ChatGPT, and do not feed it into so called "AI checkers" as they are Gen AI scrapers by another name and do not actually check anything. I grant no permissions or rights for my work to be scraped or fed into Generative AI.

About the Series

Nothing is as simple as it first appears

When her parents die from fever, Lady Sarah Montgomery Baird Watson-Wentworth has to leave India, a land she was born and raised in, and travel to England for the first time. Finding it almost impossible to adjust to London society, Sarah flees to the county of Cheshire and the country estate of Grangeback that borders the village of Stickleback Hollow.

A place filled with oddballs, eccentrics and more suspicious characters than you can shake a stick at, Sarah feels more at home in the sleepy little village than she ever did in the big city, however, even sleepy little villages have mysteries that must be solved.

Set in Victorian England, the Mysteries of Stickleback Hollow follows the crime solving efforts of Constable

Arwyn Evans, Mr. Alexander Hunter and Lady Sarah
Montgomery Baird Watson-Wentworth.

From theft to murder, supernatural occurrences and missing
people, Stickleback Hollow is a magical place filled with
oddballs, outcasts, rogues, eccentrics and ragamuffins.

About the Author

I was born in Macclesfield, Cheshire, UK, and raised in the nearby town of Wilmslow. From an early age, I discovered I had a flair and passion for writing.

I began writing at the age of 7 and was first published in 2010. I currently live in Christchurch, New Zealand.

I am an avid horsewoman and gamer, with a passion for singing, dancing, the theatre, and my garden.

Social media links: https://linktr.ee/thecswoolley

Acknowledgements

Writing can be an extremely lonely profession at times, but thankfully I never have to go through any of the pressures alone. My friends and family have been a wellspring of support that I could not have coped these past few years, and the terrible few months without.

Writing is not something I stumbled into either, my mother, Helen, took me, and my sisters, to the library every weekend when we were young to get different books, and I always maxed out the number of books I could get. Not only did she encourage me to read, but to write as well. To say I have been writing stories and poetry since I was 7 is not an exaggeration and the development of my writing career is due in no small part to her.

My mother-in-law, Lesley, has also been a source of unflinching and unwavering support, something I could not do without.

To Hollie, Frankel, and Mags, you guys are an amazing source of support and I love you all. I have known you all for so many years, you have seen me through good times and bad and have given me the drive to carry on, even in the darkest of times. Through the highs, and lows, you have been there and your friendship has always given me courage and strength.

To Holly, Dan, and Nick, who have both known me far longer than anyone else. You know my thoughts before I know them, when I am about to be incredibly stupid and when I should trust my instincts. You have driven me to search within myself for the strength I have lost over the past few years and rediscover the woman that you all love so dearly.

Dear Steve, you are a sounding board of great wisdom that is unparalleled in my life. You listen better than anyone I know and you weigh any response you give me with the greatest of care. You have been such a blessing to me and I hope that I have been an equal one to you, though I highly doubt it!

Chez, you are so dear to me and I have so enjoyed all of our experiments, plot talks, and sharing the journey of being authors together. To cheer each other on and provide understanding and an ear when others don't understand this struggle that we willingly undertake is something worth far more than any accolade or riches.

Vicki, my partner in crime, my wonderful reality check, and sounding board. You made my life in New Zealand what it is, without you it would not or could not be as amazing as it is, and I am so blessed to have you in my life.

To Ellie, you have been such a wonderful addition to my life that I hardly know where to begin or what to thank you for, but know how precious you are to me, and I will love you forever.

Courtney, you are such an incredible woman of fire and fun that I hardly know what my life was before I met you. For all the adventures to come, I know that you will make them all the more memorable by simply being you!

Karl, I have no idea how I survived before we met. Of all the people I have known and probably will ever know, you are my favourite human. The most awesome driving buddy, a constant source of support, knowledge, and helpful suggestion, my life was so much poorer before we met, and is the all the better with you in it. You've made so many things possible and helped me in more ways than I can count. I know that there is nothing I cannot do, nothing I cannot achieve, especially when   I have to try and explain to you why I can't do something. You push me when I need it most, challenge me to do better, and every day show me that I never have to settle for good enough.

And finally, to you, dear reader, without you there would be no books, no series, no career. I want to thank you for all the time that you spend reading my work, reviewing it, sharing it with your friends and family. Without you there would be nothing. Thank you from the bottom of my heart.

Until we meet again in my next book, thank you and adieu.